FOREVER HER SCOT

DUKES MOST WANTED
BOOK SIX

SCARLETT SCOTT

Forever Her Scot

Dukes Most Wanted Book Six

For more information, contact author Scarlett Scott.

https://scarlettscottauthor.com

For everyone who's been asking for Macfie's happily ever after.

CHAPTER 1

$\mathcal{M}$adeline watched in helpless despair as her friend Lady Charity Manners was led away on the capable arm of Viscount Wilton so Charity's twisted ankle could be attended by a doctor. Across a gently rolling Yorkshire field they went, the sky a brilliant blue overhead, dotted with fat, puffy clouds. The perfect, bucolic scenery was distinctly different from the massive buildings and bustling streets of Manhattan. At any other moment, Madeline might have admired the beautiful pastoral landscape of Sherborne Manor, so unlike her home in New York City.

But this moment was not an ordinary moment. Because now, Madeline was alone with the towering man at her side.

"Ye dinnae care for my presence much, do ye, lass?" he asked, his Scottish burr seemingly more pronounced than ever.

And despite her intention to remain impervious, his low, deep voice slid over her like silk velvet.

Vexed, Madeline turned her attention back to Mr. Lachlan Macfie. He was not just impossibly tall, but broad of chest and shoulder too, a massive mountain of a man who

1

was brash and disturbingly attractive, with eyes bluer than the sky and red-gold hair worn in waves that curled over his tweed coat beneath a dashing hat. He made her stomach tighten with a familiar, tingling feeling she knew to ward off whenever it arrived.

"Why do you call me *lass?*" she asked sharply.

He grinned, and the dreaded feeling returned, because that carefree sinner's smile had a most unwanted effect on her. "What else am I tae call ye?"

"Miss Chartrand." She kept her tone icy, for she recognized his sort.

Mr. Lachlan Macfie was a fortune hunter if ever she had spied one. And Miss Madeline Chartrand, daughter of one of the wealthiest men in New York City, had most certainly seen more than her fair share of fortune hunters.

Oh, he dressed the part of a gentleman quite well, aside from his brilliant hair, which was far too long to be fashionable. But all scoundrels in search of an heiress for a wife made certain to look the part. Otherwise, their schemes wouldn't be successful. They were like foxes slipping into the henhouse, greedy and dangerous.

"Miss Chartrand," he repeated, still staring at her in a way that made heat rise to her cheeks.

It was his blasted accent that affected her most, she decided. That and his height. He was a veritable giant. As a woman who was on the taller side herself, Madeline found it refreshing to converse with a man whose height surpassed hers by such a significant amount. To say nothing of the power hidden beneath his fine garments. He looked as if he were strong enough to tear a tree from the ground, roots and all, and then carry it over his shoulder like a twig.

Or to swing Madeline into his arms and whisk her away. But she didn't want that. Of course she didn't. Mr. Macfie was a fortune-hunting scoundrel.

"You should have carried Lady Charity back to the house," Madeline told Mr. Macfie, her voice curt. "You're larger and stronger than the viscount."

Rather than being duly chastened, however, Mr. Macfie's grin deepened. "I'm gratified ye noticed how strong I am, *Miss Chartrand*. However, I tried my best. Truth be told, I dinnae think Wilton wanted me tae carry his lady."

"*His* lady?" Madeline frowned, looking away.

He made her want to smile back at him.

Made her want to do more than that, in truth. Many things. Wicked things. Reckless things. Things that were foolish and stupid and would land her in a host of trouble. Which was why she couldn't afford to be alone with the man. Her own instincts weren't to be trusted. Her past attested to that; she'd nearly been duped by a silver-tongued confidence man with a beautiful smile and a penchant for saying everything she wanted to hear. She'd learned, almost too late, his true motive—not love for her as he had claimed, but an avaricious desire for her family's money.

"Aye, did ye no' notice the way he looks at her?" Mr. Macfie was saying, the words rolling from his tongue as if each syllable was a lover he caressed. "When I offered tae take her back tae the house myself, I feared Wilton would bite me like a mongrel fighting over a bone."

"That analogy is hardly complimentary to either Lord Wilton or Lady Charity." She watched the viscount and her friend disappearing into a copse of trees, wondering if she ought to chase them.

Anything to keep from being alone with the man at her side.

"'Twas a saying of my dear sainted mother's. Forgive me. I didnae intend tae pay insult."

Madeline slanted another glance in his direction to find him watching her, his good humor fading. His legs were so long, his shoulders impossibly broad. She suspected he could carry three Lady Charitys across the field without even perspiring. The muscles beneath his tweed coat were pronounced and distinctive. She found herself wondering what they would feel like, so much barely leashed strength beneath her hands.

And then she promptly banished the curiosity, for it would only lead her down a perilous road. Handsome fortune seekers were not for her. She reminded herself of their initial meeting, when Mr. Macfie had stepped on her train and spilled champagne on her silk dress. He had known who she was. He'd crowded her with his big, brawny body, heat radiating from him beneath the blazing chandeliers and making her feel quivery and faint from his proximity. He had told her she was the bonniest lass in attendance with a familiarity that had made her pulse leap.

All reasons to dislike him.

"You are forgiven the slight," she allowed reluctantly, then sighed. "Perhaps we should follow them. There's no need for a picnic now that Lady Charity has injured herself, and there's likely far too much food in the picnic hamper for two."

It didn't escape her notice that she now found herself in the sort of indecorous predicament a confidence man would take advantage of. Just herself and Mr. Macfie.

Alone.

A frisson of something wholly unwanted trilled down her spine.

And then her stupid, traitorous stomach grumbled loudly and rudely.

She pressed a hand to her middle, mortified by the noise. Mr. Macfie laughed, the sound pleasing and low.

"It seems as if yer stomach disagrees, Miss Chartrand." He

offered her his arm. "Come. We're almost tae the picnic spot I had in mind. Ye'll ken why I chose it when ye see it."

Madeline glared at his elbow, not wanting to take his arm, not wanting to accompany him a step farther. But she was hungry, her stomach reminded her with another protesting grumble. And besides, she was impervious to the devilish charm of fortune hunters. She had learned her lesson. She could endure one picnic with Mr. Lachlan Macfie unscathed.

With great reluctance, she settled her hand on his tweed coat. "Very well, Mr. Macfie. I suppose we may as well eat before we return."

What could be the harm?

Mr. Macfie smiled down at her. "Ye'll no' regret it, Miss Chartrand. That I promise ye."

As they continued up the hillside, a breeze carrying his masculine scent to her, Madeline couldn't shake the ominous feeling that she would.

IF LACHLAN MACFIE KNEW ANYTHING, it was that persuasion was always rendered easiest on a sated stomach. And that a man should never go swimming in a loch that was known for leeches. Aye, the latter was a lesson he'd learned the painful way. But it was best not to think about those wee bastards clinging to his cock, which he'd discovered in horror after finishing that ill-fated swim. His puir prick wanted to wilt and hide at the mere thought.

Which, given the state of his rampant cock whenever Miss Madeline Chartrand was in the vicinity, was probably not a bad thing at all. Because while he had a proposition for the bonny American heiress, he was decidedly keeping his prick out of it.

She was comelier than he would have preferred for his future wife. That was a temptation he surely didn't need, as he fully intended to upkeep the vow of celibacy he'd made to himself years ago. But when was he going to find another American heiress whose papa was richer than Croesus? He was running out of time, and Miss Madeline Chartrand's appearance at this house party he was attending with his friend and employer Elijah Decker had been the boon he'd been praying for ever since the cursed dukedom had fallen onto his head.

He stretched the counterpane he'd commandeered for the purpose of this blasted picnic over the ground.

Her soft voice interrupted his musings. "The wind is going to carry it away."

Lachlan was tall. Och, fair enough, he was a bloody mountain. But at the moment, he was hunched over, attempting to straighten out the blanket across the grass so that Miss Chartrand wouldn't sully her silk skirts. Which meant he had to glance up at her, craning his neck.

The sun silhouetted her form, blotted out by her dashing, flower-bedecked hat, emphasizing her lithe height and wasp waist. Her eyes were on him.

"It isnae windy," he told her, somewhat nettled that she was overseeing his progress like a mistress peering closely at her domestics as they labored beneath her lofty nose.

And then, as if to make a mockery of him, a gust of wind promptly blew the counterpane up so that it folded itself in half, ruining his efforts thus far.

"Hmm," she hummed, a noncommittal sound that bore a hint of suppressed amusement.

He scowled at the recalcitrant coverlet and then flicked a glance back in Miss Chartrand's direction. "Have ye something tae say, lass?"

"I do, in fact," she said coolly.

The airs of a queen, this one. The Americans were a peculiar lot.

"Aye?" he prompted when she didn't finish.

Miss Chartrand cocked her head, regarding him with the aloof, unaffected gaze of a lady who knew her worth—and he liked that about her, her singular, boundless confidence.

"You're calling me *lass* again."

Well, then, she'd rather caught him on that front. Miss Madeline Chartrand didn't like his familiarity. He'd been hoping she might soften toward him, rather like cold butter in the sun. Most of the lasses in his acquaintance found his unapologetic personality charming. This one was different. And mayhap that was what had drawn him to her, before he'd realized she was a hideously wealthy heiress and the answer to the most unexpected, unwanted, terrifying problem he'd faced in his life thus far. Aside from Rose, that was.

"An old habit of mine," he said lightly as he flipped the other half of the counterpane back down, moving the picnic hamper to pin it in place. "I beg yer forgiveness."

"You don't sound particularly apologetic."

Her astute observation had him hiding his smile as he smoothed the wrinkles from the coverlet. "I'm a Scot."

"Your geographical affiliation renders you incapable of contrition?" she asked tartly.

She challenged him, Miss Madeline Chartrand. And Lachlan admired her for it.

"Aye," he lied brightly. "It does."

"Hmm," she said again.

"An American word?" he teased, straightening to his full height.

He towered over her again, but Miss Madeline was tall in her own right. He liked that about her, too. And he'd be a liar if he said he hadn't thought about those long legs of hers wrapped around him more than once.

But he couldn't afford to think with any head other than the one squarely settled upon his shoulders.

"An American sound that means I don't believe you."

"Ah." He winked. "I'll have tae remember it, Miss Chartrand. All the better for our future conversations."

Her brows snapped together, and by the rood, even when she frowned at him with icy disapproval, she was lovely.

"I can't imagine we'll be having many conversations, Mr. Macfie. This house party is soon at an end."

All the more reason for him to make haste and persuade her to see the wisdom of his bargain.

He gestured toward the counterpane instead of commenting on her assertion. "Would ye care tae sit so we can fill that angry stomach of yers?"

Her blistering glare suggested her stomach wasn't the only part of her that was feeling fractious. "You do have a way with words, sir."

The manner in which she stated the observation made it clear she wasn't offering him a compliment. But never mind that. Lachlan offered her his hand to assist her in seating herself with grace—no easy feat, given the cumbersome bustle of her promenade dress. Her toilette was more suited to a ballroom than a walk through the rolling countryside of Yorkshire, but that was likely the aegis of her title-seeking mother and not the lady herself.

"I'm a Scot," he said again, as if it were an explanation for everything.

And in Lachlan's opinion, it may as well have been.

"I wouldn't have known," Miss Chartrand said dryly, taking his hand and lowering herself with unparalleled elegance to the waiting counterpane.

He caught a hint of her perfume. Roses, he thought, and

something else. Lachlan inhaled discreetly, savoring that feminine scent as a fresh burst of wind carried it to him on the air. He immediately thought better of the action. Och, he was scenting her like a hound. If he intended to charm her into accepting his bargain, he was going to have to be a gentleman.

A predicament, that.

Despite the unfortunate inheritance that had recently been foisted upon him against his will, Lachlan Macfie had never been a gentleman. Now, he was a damned duke. But that remained his secret aside from his inner circle. Guarded. Kept close, like an enemy that might stab him in the back at any moment.

When Miss Chartrand had herself settled, she released his hand as if it were a snake threatening to strike. Lachlan tried not to take too much offense at her reaction to him. He would earn her trust and make amends for the champagne incident. He'd simply have to charm the drawers off her.

Well, not literally. She could keep her drawers. Lachlan didn't even want to think about them, let alone touch them.

Clearing his throat, he took himself to the opposite end of the coverlet, a respectable distance away from her, and settled on it. By the time he was comfortable, however, it was more than apparent that his size meant he was monopolizing nearly half the blanket. If Lady Charity and Viscount Wilton had remained, there likely wouldn't have been sufficient room for both of them to sit.

It would seem that the lady's inauspicious fall had been a boon. Lord Wilton could press his suit as he escorted Lady Charity back to the manor house, and Lachlan wouldn't look a fool for bringing a coverlet that was too damned small to a picnic. With any luck, Miss Chartrand wouldn't take note of it.

"This counterpane is scarcely large enough for a picnic for four," she observed grimly, dashing all such hope.

He smiled at her. "Fortunately, it's just the right size for a picnic for two."

Her eyes narrowed, and he couldn't help but take note of the color of them—dark gray. Cool and lovely, just like the rest of her. Only, he suspected that just beneath that frosty veneer hid a great deal of fire. He'd never learn whether there was, of course. That was how he preferred it. How he *needed* it to be.

"I'm not certain if this is the result of poor planning on your part or if you somehow orchestrated this entire affair," Miss Chartrand said.

"I'm wounded." He pressed a hand to his heart, still smiling even though he suspected his levity would nettle her. "Do ye truly believe I would wish for anything ill tae befall Lady Charity? Besides, I was leading the way, if ye'll recall. How can I be responsible for the lady's fall when I wasnae anywhere near? Do ye think me a wizard, lass?"

He had called her *lass* again. Damn it, he hadn't intended to, but it rolled off his tongue so easily. He didn't ordinarily mix with polite society. Since he'd left Scotland, he had taken care to keep himself in simple circles, amongst men who worked to earn their living. Men like him. Like Elijah Decker. He didn't attend house parties and darken ballrooms with his overly large, red-headed presence. He'd never had a need. Not after Rose.

Miss Chartrand's eyes narrowed even more, attracting his attention. "I can't fathom a wizard as tall and broad as you."

"I'll consider that a compliment."

Trying not to chuckle lest he further inflame Miss Chartrand's delicate sensibilities, Lachlan bit his inner cheek and turned his attention to the picnic hamper. He unpacked plates, utensils, tumblers, a bottle each of ginger beer and lemonade, and serviettes. Next came the simple fare. A joint of cold roast beef, sliced Bayonne ham, freshly baked bread, butter and cheese, stewed fruit, strawberries, pastry biscuits, and a salad.

"It looks as if you meant to feed an army, Mr. Macfie," she observed.

"Little wonder the blessed thing was so heavy," he agreed, thinking the chef must have packed enough food for twice as many guests as he'd originally intended for this picnic. And now, their numbers had halved. "I hope ye're hungry, Miss Chartrand."

There, he hadn't called her *lass* that time. She gave no indication of whether she was pleased by the omission.

"Eager to begin our repast," she allowed, her tone suggesting even that concession had been grudging.

Lachlan retrieved the bottles of lemonade and ginger beer. "Which would ye prefer?"

"Ginger beer, please," she said primly.

"An excellent choice," Lachlan agreed easily. "Far more tae my own taste than the lemonade."

He opened the bottle and poured a generous measure into her tumbler before handing it to her. Miss Chartrand accepted it warily, her fingers brushing his. She'd removed her gloves in preparation for the picnic, and they lay neatly at her side on the counterpane. A strange sense of awareness slid through him at the contact, brief though it was. She snatched the ginger beer away with such haste that she nearly sent it sloshing over the rim of her tumbler.

Miss Chartrand had felt it too.

And she didn't like it any more than he did.

Och, well. Touching each other wasn't part of the bargain, so he needn't worry over it. Lachlan busied himself with pouring another ginger beer before settling it on a flat spot so that it wouldn't overturn and soak the blanket.

"Tell me something about yerself, Miss Chartrand," he invited as he further unpacked the provisions and took up a plate.

"Tell you something?"

"Aye. About yerself."

She eyed him as if he'd asked her to speak in an as-yet-to-be-invented language.

"Doesnae anyone ever ask ye tae do so?" he asked, frowning.

"Not gentlemen," she said, her tone thoughtful.

"There ye have it, lassie. I'm no' a gentleman." He speared a hunk of ham with a delicate fork and plopped it on the plate.

"I believe that's the salad fork." Miss Chartrand eyed his actions skeptically.

"Aye, mayhap it is. I thought it was verra small, but then when ye have paws as large as mine, *everything* is small."

He'd long since grown accustomed to the feeling that he was too large and too brutish for his surroundings. He'd simply accepted himself, such as he was: a red-haired, brawny Scot who'd never learned to hold his tongue and had more muscle than wits.

Lachlan carried on using the stupidly small fork, skewering a slice of roast beef and adding it to the plate. Next, he procured some cheese and a pastry biscuit, which he slathered with stewed fruit using a spoon that was probably also incorrect. He didn't care—ceremony wasn't for him. And the sooner Miss Chartrand learned that about him, and accepted it, the better off they'd both be.

"You've worked up an appetite," she said while he piled some fresh strawberries on the plate.

He was making a mess of it, but the sooner he had her stomach full, the sweeter she'd be. And the more amenable to his proposal.

He smiled, offering her the overflowing plate. "This isnae for me. It's for ye, Miss Chartrand."

Her eyebrows rose. "Oh dear. All that is for me? You might have asked me what I prefer."

She certainly did like taking him to task. Lachlan didn't particularly care for that. But perhaps it was an American character flaw, one which could be rectified with time and patience.

"Aye, or I could have given ye some of everything, which I've done. Except for the salad. I didnae have room for that. But the cook has given us this wee bottle of dressing, and I confess I'm partial tae lettuce. I'll just make up a second plate."

His own stomach grumbled at the prospect. The Duke and Duchess of Bradford's cook certainly knew how to craft delicious food. And Lachlan had just tramped halfway across the estate in his effort to reach the perfect spot for a picnic.

"A second plate?"

"Aye, ye ken, the one that comes after the first?" He found an angry-looking fork that was larger than the rest and used it to stab some neatly trimmed pieces of lettuce. Teasing Miss Chartrand was an excellent source of entertainment, but he mustn't grow to like her too much. That was dangerous.

"I'm well aware what the word *second* means, Mr. Macfie." Her tone was sharp again.

He took up the bottle of dressing, gave it a shake, and liberally doused her lettuce with the concoction, his mouth watering. "Merely thought tae enlighten ye, lest it was a word unfamiliar tae Americans."

"I'm reasonably certain we speak the same language." She was frowning at him again, watching him with those unusual eyes that were fringed with long, sooty lashes.

Too comely by half.

He'd best think about salad instead.

Lachlan offered her the plate of dressed lettuces. "Here ye are, Miss Chartrand."

She accepted it, settled the plate beside the first, and watched him. "Thank you."

"Now, then." He took up another plate and filled it with salad for himself. "Ye never did answer my question. Tell me something about yerself. What brought ye tae England?"

"My mother." Miss Chartrand raised her tumbler of ginger beer to her lips and took a sip. "This is quite delightful."

Lachlan knew that Mrs. William Chartrand was the reason behind her two daughters' entrance into polite society. He also knew the ginger beer was excellent; he'd been sneaking into the kitchens to beg for an extra bottle here or there whenever he could.

"Ye didnae wish tae leave America, then?" Lachlan asked before taking a long draught of his own ginger beer.

He hadn't pondered that possibility when he had settled upon his plan. The thought that Madeline Chartrand might not be amenable to remaining abroad gave him cause for alarm. He was reasonably certain he could charm the lass into his bargain, even if she was a prickly thing. But if her heart remained in New York City, the challenge would be greater than he'd anticipated.

"I didn't say that," she murmured, settling her tumbler back on the counterpane. "But my mother is the reason my sister and I are here in England. It's her most fervent wish to make aristocratic matches for us."

Lachlan took up his salad plate, unable to resist the potent lure of leafy greens and herbs drenched in the cook's decadent dressing. "It seems yer sister has made a match that will please yer mother mightily."

Miss Chartrand smiled wistfully. "Mother is quite happy

14

for Lucy to be engaged to Lord Rexingham, even if he is a mere earl. She was hoping for a duke, you see. My mother, that is, not my sister."

The mouthful of salad he'd just taken was a thing to be savored. Crisp and bright, refreshing and summery, tinged with the acidic tang of vinegar and a hint of sweetness. *Bliss.* Lachlan could have consumed the entire bowl of salad himself.

But he had more important matters to attend to.

He swallowed. "Is yer mother still hoping for a duke for ye?"

Miss Chartrand shook her head, taking a ripe red strawberry from her plate. "I should hardly think so. I've told her I have no intention of marrying."

"And why no'?" Lachlan took another bite of salad, awaiting her answer.

She nipped the very tip of her berry.

Unwanted lust reared its head inside Lachlan. There was something blatantly erotic about Miss Madeline Chartrand taking a ripe strawberry between her lips. She chewed thoughtfully, gathering her answer. He shoveled another bite of salad into his mouth to distract himself.

"Because I enjoy my independence," she announced. "Who would wish for a man to rule over them? Certainly not any woman with half her wits about her."

Her view of marriage was alarmingly grim.

"Not all men seek tae rule over their wives, as ye say," he pointed out gently. "Some men wish for equal partners."

"Ha!" She gave a bitter laugh. "Women can never be men's equals when we're denied the same rights that are bestowed upon them at birth."

She wasn't wrong, Miss Madeline Chartrand. Respect for her filled his chest with a strange tightness. He'd only known one other lass with such a strong opinion and a bold manner of speaking. But Rose didn't belong in his thoughts. She hadn't for years now. That part of his life was long gone, even if it was the reason he wanted a marriage in name only.

"A man cannae help the laws of the land, though he can try tae change them, but he *can* help the way he treats his wife," Lachlan offered.

Miss Chartrand had slipped the rest of her berry in her mouth. She finished chewing carefully. "That is quite egalitarian of you, Mr. Macfie. But also, I think, fanciful. A man can say anything he wishes before he marries. Afterward, he can change his mind, and a woman is powerless to stop him from doing whatever he likes."

"I'm a businessman, Miss Chartrand. When in doubt, always have a contract in place." Aye, he'd learned that from his years working for Decker. Along with many other lessons.

Unfortunately, none of them had involved how to be a duke. And he hadn't an inkling.

"A marriage contract, you mean?" she asked, reaching for another strawberry.

Lachlan had finished his salad, but there remained a generous portion left over, and Miss Chartrand had yet to touch hers. "Would ye care for more salad?"

Her lips twitched, as if she suppressed a smile. "No, thank you. You may finish it."

He was already using that wicked-looking fork to haul the remainder of the lettuce and herbs to his plate. "Aye, a marriage contract. No different from a business agreement, if ye think on it."

She considered him, chewing on her strawberry. "You sound like my father."

He didn't want any romantic notions between them, but neither did Lachlan want Miss Chartrand to equate him with her sire.

"Och, I'm not so auld as that," he protested after swallowing his salad and chasing it with a refreshing sip of ginger beer.

"How old are you, Mr. Macfie?" she asked.

It was the first question she'd asked him about himself, and he was ridiculously pleased by it.

"Thirty-two," he answered. "And ye, Miss Chartrand?"

"Twenty-seven."

They were only five years apart in age. He hadn't been certain, and not that it mattered overly much, but he did prefer a lass who wasn't too terribly young. The mere thought of an eighteen-year-old debutante made him want to jump into the nearest loch, leeches or no.

"I suppose it's time I apologized again about the damage I did tae yer train," he offered.

She studied him for a moment, her gaze unnerving. "You're forgiven, Mr. Macfie. My maid was able to clean the silk."

Bless her clever maid.

He finished the last bite of his salad, savoring it on his tongue before swallowing. "Thank ye for pardoning me. I'd hate tae swing from the gibbets on account of trying tae protect ye from a sneeze."

She'd taken up her plate now, apparently deciding that her pride would allow her to fully partake in the repast. "Protecting me from a sneeze, you say?"

"Aye." He leaned nearer as if he were imparting a secret. "My sneezes are as large as the rest of me. Ye'd no' have wanted tae be standing near when one came upon me. I was moving hastily tae try tae spare ye, and I spilled my champagne."

"I didn't hear a sneeze."

He grinned easily. "Aye, ye didnae. I was so horrified by ruining yer train that the sneeze disappeared."

She chuckled before compressing her lips as if she were aggrieved with herself for surrendering to levity. "I do believe you're the most interesting man I've ever met, Mr. Macfie."

Her tone suggested that wasn't a compliment.

He didn't care.

Lachlan retrieved his ginger beer and raised the tumbler to her in a toast. "Then mayhap ye'll do me the honor of becoming my wife."

Miss Madeline Chartrand's fork clattered to her plate.

CHAPTER 2

*M*arriage?

Had she heard correctly?

Had Mr. Lachlan Macfie just made a proposal of marriage to her?

Madeline stared at him, thinking she must be mistaken. Nothing in their conversation had suggested he might be interested in her romantically, let alone that he would want to *marry* her. His too-blue gaze held hers intently, the sunlight catching in his rakish hair beneath his hat, making golden strands glint. Her belly tightened, and a strange, new sense of awareness swept over her. He was looking at her expectantly.

"Mr. Macfie, I fear my ears are playing tricks on me," she said weakly.

"If ye heard me ask ye tae be my wife, then ye heard correctly." He drew one of his long legs up so he could drape his arm over his knee in a relaxed pose. "I'll admit, it wasnae the way I meant to go about it."

Understanding dawned and, with it, intense disappointment. For a few minutes there, she had been enjoying his company. His presence. She'd reluctantly fallen prey to his easy Scots charm. The way he spoke as if everything were a secret joke only the two of them were privy to, his lilting brogue, his handsome face, his big, brawny body. The way he'd consumed nearly an entire salad as if it were the world's most luxurious delicacy laid before him.

But no. She'd been fooled for a scant few, stolen seconds in time. Lachlan Macfie was everything she'd presumed him to be. And worse.

"You're a fortune hunter," she said baldly.

He winced. "Aye, Miss Chartrand. That I am—I'll no' lie. But I can explain."

Her brows rose. That was certainly different. Confidence men ordinarily didn't give away their games with such ease. Unless that, too, was a part of his plan?

"I don't think there's any need to explain," she said coolly, returning her plate to the counterpane.

Her appetite had been vanquished, her stomach soured. How had she allowed him to cozen her into believing he merely wanted her company on this picnic? A few minutes in his presence, and he'd won her over as if she were a hen being led astray by a fox. She stared at the plate of partially eaten food he had provided her, calling herself every kind of fool.

"But there *is* a need tae explain, lass."

The urgency in his tone had her glancing up at him.

She instantly regretted it, for his countenance was earnest. She couldn't look away.

Madeline swallowed hard. "Explain, then. I see dark clouds on the horizon. We should pack up this picnic and return to the manor house before we're caught in a deluge."

In truth, she didn't see any dark clouds. But the urge to

escape this man's unsettling presence was strong. She had to put some distance between them before he persuaded her he wasn't a villain and that he had an admirable reason for wanting to seize her dowry.

"Forgive me for tripping over my tongue. It's no' every day I ask a lass tae marry me, ye ken."

"I should hope not," she said crisply. "As that would rather ruin the singularity of such an occasion."

"In fact, this is only the second time I've ever asked a lass tae marry me," he continued, frowning as if he were recalling the first instance.

Judging from his countenance, it hadn't been a happy occasion. But it wasn't only his reaction that affected her, in spite of herself. It was also the notion of him wanting to marry someone else that bothered Madeline. And she couldn't precisely say why. Pride, perhaps.

"Should I be insulted that I'm merely your second choice?" she asked cuttingly.

"Och." He scrubbed his hand along his chiseled jaw, which was covered with a light stubble of red-gold whiskers. Not a true beard, but enough of a shadow for it to be plain he hadn't shaved in several days. "I'm going about this all wrong. The first time was many years ago. I was young, and so was the lass."

Curiosity prompted another question, once more against her better judgment. "Did she accept?"

A muscle clenched in his jaw. "She didnae."

And her refusal had caused him pain, Madeline realized. Still caused him pain, it would seem. Not that it mattered to her either way. She had no intention of marrying this man. Of marrying any man, for that matter, as she'd so recently told him.

"I regretfully inform you that I'm not any more inclined

to accept your kind proposal than my predecessor was," she told him. "Now, we really ought to see to the plates and food."

"Will ye no' hear what I have tae offer ye first?" He was frowning at her, still rubbing his jaw with one massive hand.

And for a wild moment, she thought about how that hand of his might feel on her. Stroking her own jaw, cupping her cheek. Gliding over her neck. Holding her nape.

No. What was she thinking? She wasn't attracted to this Scottish brute who had just admitted he was a fortune hunter. Why, he was no better than Charles had been. Only, Charles had kept his true motives from her until it had been almost too late. She'd avoided disaster then, and she would avoid it again now.

"I don't think it would be wise, Mr. Macfie."

She glared down at her plate, bemused to find her stomach growling again as she took in the pastry biscuit covered in stewed fruit, the Bayonne ham, the roast beef, the cheese. She'd eaten nothing more than a few berries, and she was still famished, curse it all.

"It would seem yer stomach is yer enemy once again," he rumbled, sounding faintly amused.

"If you were a gentleman, you wouldn't comment on it."

"Aye, but I'm no' a gentleman. We've already discussed my shortcomings." There was a smile in his voice that had her glancing up to find him watching her. "But while I may no' be a gentleman, I *am* a duke."

She stared at him. "I believe I'm acquainted enough with the vagaries of your customs here to understand that a mister can't be a duke."

"Aye, he can be if he inherited a dukedom and he hasnae told anyone—save his closest friends—about it just yet."

Interesting.

Madeline studied him for any signs of prevarication. He held her gaze without blinking.

"A duke," she echoed. "You?"

"Me." He gave her a wry grin. "Believe me, lass, it's with the greatest of reluctance that I've had tae realize there's no escaping my fate. I was fifth in line tae inherit, and yet here I sit before ye, the next Duke of Kenross."

Now she didn't know what she ought to call him. Your Grace? Duke? Kenross? Mr. Macfie?

She frowned. "Why haven't you told everyone you're the Duke of Kenross?"

"Because I've been trying tae avoid it." He sighed heavily. "I like the life I've built for myself here. But I cannae avoid it any longer. I've inherited a mountain of debt, a dilapidated castle, and people who need me tae look after them. That's where ye come in, Miss Chartrand. Or rather, yer dowry."

"You want to marry me to pay off the debt you've inherited and restore your dilapidated castle," she said, rather wounded he hadn't wished to marry her for another reason.

One that had more to do with Madeline herself than with her family's fortune.

"Aye," he agreed. "I do."

"An excellent plan." She flicked at an imaginary crumb on her skirt to hide her disappointment, which was as silly as it was irrational. "But I fail to see what your need of my dowry has to do with me. Indeed, your proposal seems suspiciously one-sided."

Not anything she wasn't accustomed to, of course.

"Ye want yer freedom," he said. "Yer mother wants ye tae marry a title. I'm a duke. I'll have a marriage contract drawn up that gives ye anything ye ask for. It'll be the answer tae both our problems. An easy solution."

"Surely not so easy if I have to agree to a marriage I don't want," she pointed out.

"The marriage I offer ye isnae quite like an ordinary one. It will be a marriage in name only."

His words gave her pause. "In name only?"

"Aye. I'll no' make any demands of ye in regard tae the marriage bed. A chaste marriage is all I'm after, lass. Well, that and yer dowry. As for the rest, ye'll be free tae do whatever ye like. Travel where ye wish, do what pleases ye. Ye'll be a free woman, only ye willnae have tae answer tae yer mother or anyone else. No' even me."

The marriage he proposed was quite unusual. She'd heard of marriages of convenience, of course. New York society marriages were notoriously cold-blooded. She knew that alliances were often made between a man and a woman for reasons other than love—money and éclat chief amongst them. But she'd never heard of a chaste marriage. At least, not anywhere other than in gossip and rumors.

"What you're proposing is my dowry in exchange for the freedom I already possess?" She shook her head. "Forgive me, but it hardly seems an equal trade."

"But are ye *truly* free, lass? It seems tae me that both ye and yer sister are at the whims of yer mother, who's been trotting ye about London like a pair of thoroughbreds she intends tae auction off."

Her shoulders stiffened, her spine straightening. His words were far too close to the mark.

"You ought to watch your tongue, sir. I don't recall inquiring after your opinion on my mother's marital aspirations for either myself or Lucy."

"Ye didnae, but I can plainly see they aren't making ye happy."

They weren't, and she resented him for taking note. Marrying an aristocrat had never been Madeline's dream. Nor had it been Lucy's, even if she was left with no choice but to wed the earl after their unfortunate tryst in the midnight gardens, followed by the gossipmonger Lady Featherstone's discovery of the two of them in a heated embrace. Now that Madeline thought upon it, perhaps her sister wouldn't find marriage such a dreadful fate after all. She certainly did seem smitten with the earl, even if she was fighting it.

"It's hardly any of your concern whether I'm happy," she snapped. "I'm afraid my answer to your proposal must be no."

A sound, firm no.

"Are ye certain, lass?"

Of course she was certain. Why would she marry a penniless Scottish duke when she could carry on perfectly well as she was, without a man to answer to and dictate her fate? Eventually, Mother would tire of her campaign to see both her daughters married. Indeed, Madeline already had hope that Lucy's impending nuptials would prove sufficient distraction for their mother. That landing one of her daughters an earl and orchestrating what she'd decreed would be the marriage of the century would be enough of a feather in Mother's cap without Madeline having to sacrifice herself.

"I'm certain," she confirmed, gentling her tone to take some of the sting from her refusal. "I'm sorry, but a marriage between us would never be what I wanted for myself."

She had escaped one fortune hunter's trap, and she wasn't about to throw herself into another. Even if he was a devastatingly handsome Scot with an accent like velvet to her senses, a grin that made her want to smile back at him, and the broadest shoulders she'd ever seen.

"I cannae change yer mind?"

"No," Madeline told him firmly. "You cannot."

"Och." He rubbed his jaw, giving her a rueful grin. "Ye cannae fault a man for trying. Let's at least finish this fine picnic before we return tae the manor house. It would be a shame for it tae go tae waste."

Her protesting stomach agreed.

Their picnic resumed, and Madeline steeled herself against the new Duke of Kenross's undeniable Scottish charm.

~

"ARE FELICITATIONS IN ORDER?" Decker asked Lachlan later that evening as they squared off in a game of billiards.

Lachlan shook his head, heaving a sigh. "The lass doesnae want tae marry me."

"No? And why not, with you being such a fine matrimonial catch?" his friend and employer teased, taking aim and delivering a clean shot. "She didn't mention your eyebrows in her refusal, did she?"

"Och, leave my puir eyebrows out of this." Lachlan chuckled despite himself, for Decker had been mocking his eyebrows for as long as he could recall.

Their friendship was easy. Lachlan owed Elijah Decker his life. He'd left Scotland years earlier, adrift and uncertain of what he wanted. Fifth in line and a lifetime away from a dukedom. Far from the woman he'd wanted to spend the rest of his life with and have by his side—the woman who had thrown him over for another and crushed his heart. Decker had been building his already impressive empire then. He'd hired Lachlan on, and Lachlan had suddenly been given a new purpose. A driving force to bring him out of the darkness where Rose had left him.

Not that he'd ever shared the full truth of his past with Decker, or the state it had left him in. What he'd endured was too painful to dredge up, regardless of how close he was to his friend. Decker had never questioned the lack of female companionship in Lachlan's bed or the reason for it. Knowing his friend as he did, Lachlan suspected Decker would have thought him mad for forgoing physical relationships. But he'd never been capable of separating emotions from lovemaking the way some men could.

"Not the eyebrows, then." Decker raised a brow, his gaze searching. "Why did she refuse? I would have thought Miss Chartrand would eagerly agree to escape her matchmaking mama's clutches."

"Apparently I'm no' a sufficient catch," he drawled grimly.

Aye, he was aware that a largely unknown Scottish dukedom deep in debt hardly presented an attractive future for a spoiled, beautiful heiress who could have her choice of any husband she wanted. But he'd been hoping she might find sufficient reason to accept his offer just the same. Because he was running out of time, and because finding a wealthy wife at this house party would have been the answer to all his problems. Well, not *all* his problems. Just the one that was currently threatening to crush him beneath its omnipotent weight.

"You could do as I did and kidnap your bride," the Earl of Sinclair offered, grinning as he raised his glass of brandy in a mock toast.

Tall, dark-haired, and bearing a general air of menace, the earl was known for his dangerous reputation. The rumors that he'd killed his first wife had certainly added to the mystique. He'd long been friends with Decker, and Lachlan had befriended him as well over the years. These days, the earl was a happily married man just like Decker, a lion turned into a kitten.

Lachlan turned his attention to the baize, taking aim. "Miss Chartrand is an American. If I tried tae kidnap her, she'd likely shoot me in the arse."

"Only if you give her the opportunity, my good man," Sinclair countered.

"The way to a lady's heart is paved with cream ice," Decker interrupted as Lachlan scored a point.

"Och, 'tis a wonder ye havenae turned tae cream ice by now," Lachlan grumbled good-naturedly.

Decker was known for spoiling his beloved wife, and that often involved plying her with cream ices. Lachlan himself had fetched her favorite flavors on more than one occasion.

"Women want to be wooed," Decker told him with feeling. "They want to be seduced."

"They do," Sinclair agreed, nodding. "Have you courted the lady in question?"

"Courted her?" Lachlan snorted. "I dinnae court."

He had once, but he tamped down that thought with brutal ferocity.

Decker snorted, casting Sinclair a wry look as he took aim again. "As *you* courted Lady Sinclair? Ha!"

"I did court her," Sinclair defended himself, frowning. "After we married. And I'll have you know that she fell in love with me quite soundly."

"Against her better judgment, no doubt," Decker teased his friend, grinning as he scored a point for himself. "To say nothing of all ration and reason."

"She ought to have run screaming in the opposite direction," the earl agreed easily. "Fortunately for me, she stayed."

Lachlan took his turn, finding it difficult to concentrate. Despite his best attempts at aiming, he missed Decker's ball, ceding the point to his friend. It seemed rather representative of his earlier efforts where Miss Madeline Chartrand was concerned.

"Forgive me for saying the obvious, but I dinnae find either of ye tae be reliable sources of advice when it comes tae winning a woman."

True, Decker and Sinclair were both happily wedded men who were deliriously in love with their wives. But that was the point. Lachlan didn't want a love match. He didn't want to woo a woman and win her heart. He didn't want seduction and niceties and cream ice. He wanted a woman who would help him to look after his people and the land he'd unexpectedly inherited.

"I'm wounded." Sinclair pressed a hand to his heart, his expression schooled into melodramatic sadness more suited to the stage than an earl swilling brandy in the billiards room.

"I'm of half a mind to give you the sack for the insult," Decker said without bite, grinning at him as he took aim and scored another point, well on his way to victory.

And that, too, was suiting. It would seem Lachlan was destined to lose at every endeavor he tried his hand at today.

"Fortunately, I've inherited a penniless dukedom and a derelict castle," Lachlan replied dryly. "I havenae any need for yer position."

Decker sobered. "You know I'm more than happy to give you anything you need. Wife hunting isn't necessary."

Decker was generous. More generous than he ought to be. But Lachlan couldn't accept alms from anyone. Becoming the next Duke of Kenross was an albatross he'd have to shoulder alone rather than drag down his friend.

"I dinnae want a loan, but I thank ye," Lachlan said, taking aim and missing his objective. "Damn and blast, I havenae any luck at all today."

Or ever. But never mind that.

"I'm not speaking of a loan," Decker said quietly. "I'm talking about a gift in return for all your years of service and friendship."

"Charity," Lachlan scoffed. "I'm grateful for the offer, but nay. I'll no' take that any more than I would a loan from ye. This problem is mine tae solve, and that's that."

His pride wouldn't allow it. He thought again of the lovely Miss Chartrand. Of how her eyes sparkled in the sun and her long legs could keep pace with his. Of how her delicate floral scent had carried to him on the breeze, wrapping around him in subtle invitation. Of how full and inviting and lush her lips were. Of how bold and direct she was, her defiance a mantle she wrapped around herself as if it were the finest Parisian habit. She would have suited his purpose quite fine as a wife. But it wasn't meant to be. He'd simply have to settle for someone else.

Perhaps someone whose dowry wasn't nearly as massive.

But even a small fortune would do wonders to restore Kenross Castle. At least, he hoped it would. There were other unattached ladies in attendance. Perhaps he could persuade one of them to wed him.

"You might have better luck with finding a lady to marry you if you let it be known that you're the new Duke of Kenross," Sinclair suggested, before taking a pensive sip of his brandy. "We all know how the ladies adore dukes."

"Och, aye, but do they love overly tall Scottish dukes with uninhabitable castles who are in desperate need of an heiress?" Lachlan queried grimly.

He wasn't accustomed to being a duke.

To being Kenross.

It was a title he'd never aspired to, and one he most certainly never should have inherited, given how distantly he'd been related to the previous duke. Lachlan was last in line; the title was so ancient and moldering that there was no one to take it on after him. He intended to do his duty to the people and land that had become his responsibility. But beyond that, the title could go rot.

He was Lachlan Macfie first, damn it, and the Duke of Kenross second.

"Don't forget the bit about slamming doors and not knowing your own strength," Decker added, grinning.

"Point well taken," the earl said agreeably, raising his brandy in another salute. "Now, if you don't mind, Decker, finish trouncing the Scot so I can have my turn at giving you the drubbing you deserve."

"You'll never win against me," Decker warned smugly, taking aim and scoring yet another point, which left him perilously near to victory. "I'm the undisputed king of billiards."

"King of *something* is what ye are." Lachlan couldn't resist teasing his friend.

"King of what?" Decker asked with mock outrage. "Are you trying to tell me something, old chum? And here I am, on my best behavior, attempting to offer moral support and guidance, et cetera."

"Ha, the only best behavior ye have is when ye're sleeping." Lachlan grinned.

He missed his mark yet again, his own ball landing in the pocket and handing Decker a victory.

"My behavior is exemplary at all times," his friend countered. "Just ask my wife."

"I'll be sure no' tae do that," Lachlan said, surrendering his cue stick. "The puir dear lady is so in love with ye that she cannae see yer many faults."

"As is the duty of every good wife," the earl said amiably, taking up the cue. "They're saints and angels for enduring us."

Lachlan knew a brief pang of envy for the way his friends spoke of their wives with unabashed admiration and love. Once, long ago, he had hoped to marry and have half a dozen bairns and live in unbridled happiness. Once, he'd been young and naïve and foolish enough to think that Rose had loved him as deeply as he'd loved her. When it had come down to it, she hadn't loved him at all. But that hardly mattered now as she was another man's wife. And he was about to marry another woman.

Not Miss Madeline Chartrand, alas.

But the next lass he could find and persuade to take him on.

With all haste.

CHAPTER 3

*M*adeline wasn't dressed for rain or for an impromptu tour of castle ruins. But as the sky opened and began to unleash a fresh deluge around her, she conceded that she hadn't much choice other than to seek shelter in the long-abandoned castle nestled in the woods at Sherborne Manor. Catching her walking gown in both hands as she hastened through the overgrown bailey to the mossed-over walls of the centuries-old edifice, she slipped into the first area she could find that still bore a roof rather than a hole to the sky.

The walls were cold and dank, and the lack of light had her imagining all manner of massive spiders and other dreadful creatures hiding in the shadows, prepared to bite her. A shiver went down her spine as she walked into a wall of cobwebs, the sticky substance in her hair and on her face.

"Damnation," she cursed, frantically scrubbing at her cheek.

She was growing incredibly weary of this house party. It seemed that with each passing day, Madeline's own luck grew worse. With Lucy's imminent marriage to the Earl of

Rexingham settled, Mother was not content to plan one daughter's wedding. Oh, no. This morning at breakfast, she had begun placing a great deal of pressure on Madeline to make a match as well.

Not just pressure either. She had issued an ultimatum that had come through telegram directly from Father. Madeline had two months to marry or her father would choose a husband for her himself from amongst the sons of his New York business associates.

To say she'd been horrified at the prospect would have been a vast understatement. Madeline knew those men. They were the sort who wanted a Chartrand on their arm for the social status, wealth, and connection it would bring them. Madeline herself didn't have a thing to do with it. Such a marriage would be every bit as cold as the one Mr. Macfie had proposed. No, she mustn't think of him as Mr. Macfie now, but rather as the Duke of Kilnross. Or was it Glenross?

She'd already forgotten.

Feeling grim, Madeline heaved out a sigh, watching the rain pelt the earth from beyond her sheltered haven. And that was when she heard the undeniable sound of something large moving toward her, the rustle rising above the loud din of rain and clapping thunder overhead. But it wasn't just movement she heard. It was also the menacing sound of something...*snarling.*

What could it be? A wolf? A bear? Did Yorkshire have bears and wolves? Was it a mountain lion or a deer? What manner of animal would produce such prodigious sound? She had no notion of what mysteries lurked in the wilds of England. Heavens, she didn't even know what lurked in the wilds of her home state, because she scarcely ever left the familiar city that had been her home since birth.

A tremor of trepidation went down Madeline's spine as she held her breath, waiting for the creature to venture into her line of sight. Although she had been on a walk with a gathering of many others from the house party, she'd become separated from them when she'd wandered off in the direction of the looming castle ruins in the distance, bored with the niceties and conversations surrounding her. Not even the lure of learning more about the Lady's Suffrage Society had proven sufficient impetus for her to linger. She'd been curiously inspecting the outer walls of the old castle just as a fresh storm had rolled over the horizon, effectively trapping her.

But as far as she knew, she was alone. No one had followed her to the castle, and she had no notion of how much time had passed since she had become separated from the others. It was entirely likely that they had all already returned to the main house, leaving her out here alone. In the storm.

With whatever lumbering beast was growing closer.

Good heavens, was that a growl she heard? What if it was some sort of ravenous wild animal, hell-bent upon tearing her apart and eating her for its dinner? What if it sank its massive teeth into her and she couldn't escape? She had to do something. To protect herself if she was able.

The sounds came nearer, and Madeline looked wildly about for something she might use as a weapon. In the dank shadows, she spied what appeared to be a large branch.

Bending, she seized it in her hands and swung around, heart beating fast and hard as the steps crunched ever nearer. Pressing herself against the wall, she held her breath, waiting until the right moment. Just as the footfalls grew close to the moldering interior room where she had taken shelter, she leapt into the doorway, swinging the heavy branch in her hands wildly, employing all the force she could muster.

Her branch connected with an impossibly large, shadowy figure that loomed in the doorway. Dear sweet heavens, it *was* a bear! Madeline knew a moment of instant relief at the satisfying thud of her branch meeting enemy flesh, along with the startled howl of pain. She'd likely done it at least a little harm, but she wasn't finished yet.

She pulled back the branch a second time, intending to beat the beast into submission if it was the last action she took on this earth. She, Madeline Chartrand of the New York Chartrands, daughter of Mr. William Chartrand, American heiress celebrated in the newspapers for her beauty on both sides of the Atlantic, was not going to become the unwitting supper of some English grizzly bear!

She swung her branch again, but this time, the shadow moved toward her, taking her weapon from her with ease and...fingers.

"Sweet Jesus, woman," complained the looming shadow in a smooth Scottish burr rendered hard around the edges by outrage. "That smarted."

The masculine growl was unmistakable.

Oh dear.

She pressed a hand over her racing heart, her fingers nerveless from her fright. "Mr. Macfie...Your Grace...is that you?"

"Och, of course it's me, lass." He dropped the branch he'd taken from her to the ground, rubbing his shoulder, the light from behind him and her scattered fear making her see him more clearly now. "Who did ye think I was?"

"A grizzly bear."

He laughed, the sound so loud that she gave another start, his levity echoing off the walls of the confined space. "A grizzly bear, ye say?"

And what did he find so amusing?

Madeline bristled. "You scared me half to death, you know."

He chuckled some more, which was vastly irritating to

Madeline, because she found the sound of his laughter disturbingly pleasant. After the fear that had just set her teeth on edge and left her dry-mouthed and with her heart pounding, the discovery was a most unwelcome one.

"What is so funny?" she demanded as his laughter continued.

At her expense, she thought peevishly.

"We dinnae have grizzly bears here, lass," he said, humor lacing his rumbly voice.

"You don't?" She glared at him through the darkness as thunder roared overhead in an ominous crack and the rain poured down harder beyond their sheltered alcove.

"Nay, lass." He rubbed at his jaw with one of his large hands. "And I know I'm tall, but I cannae say I've ever been mistaken for a bear before."

"How was I to know what manner of creatures are running wild through your woodland?" she demanded, heat rising to her cheeks.

She felt unutterably foolish.

"Do ye have red-haired bears in America?" he asked, his voice softened with a teasing air.

"I wouldn't think so." She huffed out a sigh of irritation. "What are you doing here in the castle ruins? I thought I was alone."

"Actually, ye thought ye were with a bear."

His amusement made something inside her snap. Perhaps it was the vast changes unfolding in her life—her sister suddenly about to marry, so many of her friends getting engaged. Perhaps it was her mother's stubborn insistence that she wed, or her father's unsettling demand that she marry in the next two months or find herself forever bound to a man of his choosing. Or perhaps it was even her own unexpected, nettling reaction to the overgrown Scot who found her ignorance so dratted amusing.

Whatever the cause, Madeline needed time. Space. Needed to be alone.

So she whirled about without further word or thought and stalked deeper into the darkness of the castle, finding a narrow passage that led her away from the chamber where she'd sought temporary shelter from the storm.

"Lass?"

His voice trailed after her, still tinged with amusement. But Madeline ignored him. It didn't matter that it was dark and she could scarcely find her way. Or that more cobwebs plastered themselves to her hair and face. Or that the ceiling was sloped and dreadfully low overhead. She was escaping his maddening presence, his laughter, his...

Him, damn it. She was escaping *him*.

"Lass, dinnae go any farther," he cautioned. "The castle likely isnae stable enough."

"It's been here for centuries, has it not?" she asked dismissively over her shoulder. "I'll be fine. And besides, I distinctly recall telling you to refrain from calling me lass."

"Miss Chartrand, then," he corrected, the sound of his booted footfalls crunching after her, exasperation now lacing his Scots burr. "Come back, if ye please. 'Tis dangerous."

The only thing that was truly dangerous was lingering in his overly large presence a moment longer than necessary. Because she liked the way her name sounded when he said it with his deep, velvety voice. Because she liked the way his massive height, broad chest, and masculine strength made her feel small and dainty in a way other gentlemen of her acquaintance never had.

Because some part of her was desperately attracted to Lachlan Macfie, despite the fact that he had spilled champagne on her gown, trampled her train, offered her a marriage in name only, and now laughed at her lack of knowledge when it came to England's fauna. Truly, how was she to have known they didn't have grizzly bears here?

The sheer daring of the man! He was maddening. Irritating. Infuriating.

Handsome.

No, not that. Lengthening her strides, she stomped forward, allowing her displeasure free rein.

"Miss Chartrand, wait."

He was still following her, curse the man. Madeline went faster. Deeper into the darkness. Following the narrow, dank-smelling passageway despite her own misgivings about the lack of light and the wisdom of traveling into the heart of the dilapidated castle. Grimly, she wondered if this was what his castle in Scotland looked like. And then she promptly banished the curiosity, foolish as it was.

His ramshackle Scottish castle meant less than nothing to her. She'd never see it. And after this house party, she'd never see *him* again. Another ominous clap of thunder sounded overhead, followed by a flash of lightning that briefly lit up the passage. Nothing but stone walls and a dirty stone floor. For some reason, she had always imagined that castles were enchanted fortresses, filled with lovely furnishings and handsome knights.

But she'd likely been reading too many novels that swept her away to fanciful settings.

A crack sounded suddenly, loud and just overhead.

"Lass, dinnae go—"

His worried call was abruptly drowned out by a crashing sound. Everything happened at once. Something struck the outer castle wall with tremendous force. Stones rained overhead. A portentous quiet filled the air as she stood, panicked, not knowing what to do next, the fear that she had so recently chased off rising to prominence once more.

And then, the passageway began to cave in on itself.

Rocks tumbled around her, atop her, darkness truly descending. She screamed and huddled into a ball, throwing her arms over her head.

~

By God.

The castle was crumbling around Miss Chartrand.

Lachlan didn't think twice. Didn't spare a thought for his own welfare. He charged forward through a hail of raining debris and threw himself atop her cowering form. In the darkness, he managed to find her somehow, the soft, pliant body beneath him trembling with fear. Lightning must have struck a nearby tree, felling it. And the tree had fallen into the castle wall, which had, in turn, collapsed into the passageway.

Everything made sense as stone rained down around him, atop him, burying them. It was as if an avalanche had been unleashed. But instead of snow, it was centuries' worth of castle rock giving way. He grunted beneath the weight and strain of it, pain slicing through him as rocks hammered his back and skull. But through the onslaught, he remained determined and strong, using his massive frame to shelter Miss Chartrand.

Until at last, all was quiet again, save for the rain continuing to fall and the rumble of thunder fading into the distance.

"Lass," he managed to grind out, balanced atop her as if he were a table, on his hands and knees. "Are ye hurt?"

"I'm... No. I don't think so." Her voice was muffled and small.

And the tremor of terror he heard within it made something inside him seize.

"Stay where ye are," he ordered her. "Dinnae move. I'm

covered in rocks, but I'll do the best I can tae get us both out of here."

"D-did the wall fall on you?" she asked.

Och. He had what felt like the weight of the entire bloody castle on his back, and she wanted to ask questions.

"We'll talk later, lass," he growled out. "For now, what matters most is seeing ye out of this rubble safely."

And himself too. The challenge would be to find the strength to move without further dislodging the stones surrounding them. He'd be damned if he would send any to fall atop her after managing to protect her from the worst of the collapse.

"Yes," she said, agreeable and meek for the first time since he'd met the stunning American heiress.

He missed her fire.

"Remain still," he reminded her, tamping down a groan at the strain on his aching back. "I'm going tae shift and see if I can get some of these blasted rocks pushed tae the side. Tell me if anything falls on ye or if ye're hurt in any way."

"I can help," she offered, shifting beneath him, her knee connecting with his thigh.

"*Dinnae. Move,*" he ground out sharply.

"O-of course."

Carefully, he shifted the burden of his weight to his left arm, slowly freeing up his right. He hefted a stone, moving it along the pile so that it rolled away from them. Sweat trickled down his brow, running into his eye and making it sting. He blinked it furiously away and carried on, stone by stone, systematically removing the weight that had piled on the right side of him, until his arm trembled from the weight of the rocks yet upon his back.

Grunting, he braced his right palm flat on the stone floor again, then transferred his weight so that he could use his left arm to begin clearing rocks from that side as well. With painstaking concentration and sheer determination, Lachlan hefted them one by one, taking care to make sure that the rubble didn't roll back atop them or further cave in. He was keenly aware of the precariousness of their position. They were still flanked in shadows and darkness, the portion of the castle wall that had crumbled atop them keeping them sheltered from the rain but also keeping them in danger of being buried by a fresh wave of rocks.

Thank God the entire castle wall hadn't given in, or they would have been crushed to death. As it was, they were both in desperate peril of being trapped, severely injured, or worse. Grunting against the twinges of pain in his back, he worked more stones free, carving out a space that enabled him to move while keeping Miss Chartrand safe beneath his big body. For once, his tremendous size had proven a boon.

After what seemed a lifetime of careful, slow movement, of rolling rocks away and making certain to keep them from falling back atop himself or her, Lachlan had freed himself enough that he could move to the side, giving Miss Chartrand a path to safety.

"I'm going tae move tae my right, lass," he told her. "When I tell ye tae go, ye'll need tae move out of here with as much haste as ye can manage. Are ye able tae move?"

"I… Yes," she said. "I believe so."

Her voice still held the undeniable tone of fear.

He hated hearing it. But he had no time to linger on that thought. More rocks gave way from the wall that had partially crumbled, sending another hefty stone rolling down. Lachlan caught the brunt of it with his shoulder. He had to act quickly and get her out of this blasted corridor before the rest of the wall caved in on them both, sealing them in their tomb.

He shifted, creating a safe space, using his body, his

weight, and all the muscle he possessed to hold the rocks at bay, giving her access to the corridor that had yet to collapse.

"Go now, lass," he ordered. "Dinnae hesitate."

"But what about you?" she asked, scrambling under him.

"Dinnae worry about me. Just get yerself out of here before one of these rocks crushes yer pretty heid. Tell me when ye're in the main room."

"But—"

"Go," he interrupted roughly, not sure how much longer he could withstand the pressure of the rocks that threatened to crumble around him.

The sound of her scraping and crawling across the stone floor reached him. He waited what felt like an eternity, praying he'd sufficiently freed her so that she could escape, until she finally called to him that she'd made it to the more secure area of the castle. And then carefully, with excruciating torpor, he moved himself. Inch by inch, slowly leveraging his body away from the partially fallen wall. As he went, more rocks caved in, filling the space where Miss Chartrand had been. With the last strength he had, he heaved himself backward, landing with a painful thud on his back as the walls of the corridor shifted and slipped, caving in on each other.

"Mr. Macfie! Your Grace!"

Miss Chartrand was there, hovering over him, her hair having come loose from its confines to trail down over his cheeks, tickling him. Lachlan lay there for a dazed moment, scarcely aware he'd just saved them both from imminent death, his muscles weak and on fire, his back aching from where he had absorbed the blows and the weight of the falling wall.

They were still within the narrow corridor she'd disappeared down in her fit of pique just before the lightning had felled the tree. It wasn't safe.

"We need tae get ourselves out of this corridor, lass," he managed. "It isnae safe."

As if on cue, the rattle of more stones coming loose echoed around them.

"Can you stand?" she asked, desperation in her tone. "Are you injured?"

"I'm spent, is all," he said, heaving himself into a sitting position and then standing, hunched over to keep from hitting his head on the low ceiling. "I used every bit of my strength tae keep those blasted rocks from crushing us both."

"You saved my life."

Her voice bore a hushed reverence steeped in gratitude. Lachlan couldn't lie. He rather liked the sound of it. Liked being the recipient. Liked the notion of the lass who had turned down his marriage proposal yesterday suddenly thinking him her savior.

But now wasn't the time to bask in the glow of her adulation. They had to get their arses out of this damned corridor before the rest of the walls came tumbling down, making a mockery of the disaster they'd just narrowly averted.

"Come, lass," he said, grasping her hand in the shadows and pulling the both of them from the hall.

Just in time.

The roof of the area that had been standing collapsed behind them, almost as if it had been suddenly turned to dust. They scarcely escaped through the door into the outside world, where the sun was attempting to make an appearance from behind the dark gray clouds. It was still raining lightly, but they could see. They had escaped from certain death.

They faced each other, their breathing mutually ragged. Miss Chartrand was missing her hat. Her chignon was partially undone, and her chestnut locks were falling wildly around her face. Her cheeks were covered in dust, and as the drizzle continued to fall, it kissed her cheeks, gently cleansing them of the dirt. He knew he likely looked akin to the grizzly bear she had originally believed him to be. He was probably mussed and dirtied, covered in dust and sweat. But he didn't care. Lachlan had never been happier to see the leaden Yorkshire sky, to feel his heart thudding in his chest.

He stared down at Miss Chartrand in new wonder, a potent surge of relief washing over him like the rain. She was beautiful. And they were alive. Relatively unscathed. But *alive*. Aye, his back ached, his arms would likely be bruised on the morrow from his endeavors. But they hadn't been crushed to death beneath the weight of the castle walls.

Somehow, they'd survived.

It was a miracle.

She was a miracle. A gray-eyed, bedraggled, beautiful, stubborn, sharp-tongued, sultry-lipped American siren. Their hands were still linked. Her fingers tightened on his. Something changed in the air around them, between them. He pulled her into his chest before he could even properly think about the ramifications. With his other hand, he cupped her cheek, using the pad of his thumb to trace her cheekbone, swiping at the raindrops that were clinging to her dewy skin.

And then he did the unthinkable. His head dipped, his mouth sealing over hers. He kissed her. Swiftly, soundly. Chastely at first. Victory over death was roaring through his veins, overwhelming his mind. All he knew was that he needed to celebrate. To revel in their shared survival. He needed her lips.

They were soft and lush and full.

And hot.

Wet from rain.

Forbidden.

He shouldn't be kissing her. This was an aberration. His rudimentary instinct taking command of his faculties and making him do things he ordinarily wouldn't. But then she made a sound from low in her throat. A sound of need, of surrender. And he was lost. He parted her lips with his, kissed her more fully.

Their tangled fingers fell apart, and she wound her arms around his neck. She pressed herself against him, sending the lush give of her curves into his hardness until his cock was somehow throbbing, springing stiff and erect, burrowing into her skirts. He'd never in his life managed to get a cockstand in such circumstances. But then, when had he ever cheated death before?

And when had he ever kissed a woman who responded the way Madeline Chartrand did?

Never.

The answer spurred him on. He was weak; he was the beast she'd believed him to be. He wrapped her in his arms, holding her tightly, and drank from her mouth as if it were his life source. She made another sound, and when she opened for him and his tongue slipped into her mouth, her tongue glided against his in answering welcome.

She tasted sweet, like sugar and tea with a hint of cream. Mysterious. Clean, like rain, and earthy too. He sank his fingers into her hair. It was silken and long and heavy, slightly damp from the rain, and, despite the way she'd just been buried in dusty rubble, still smelled delightfully like roses and fresh soap and woman.

He was lost.

He was found.

Lachlan could kiss this woman forever, and it would never be enough.

Nay, what was he thinking? He couldn't kiss her forever.

He shouldn't even be kissing her now. Shouldn't have kissed her at all. She'd turned down his proposal. And he didn't dally with women. He'd been celibate as a monk since Rose had thrown him over. He had no intention of changing that. No intention of allowing a woman to get past his defenses and lay him low ever again.

It was raining.

His prick was harder than marble.

Heaven and hell and all that was holy. This was wrong. What was the matter with him?

Lachlan lifted his head, tearing his mouth from hers, staring down at her, struggling for breath, but for a different reason. One that had less to do with their escape from the collapsing castle walls and far more to do with the woman in his arms.

She looked up at him, eyes glazed with passion, rain still falling all around them, and he couldn't help himself. He lowered his head and took her lips again. Softer this time. With greater care. And she kissed him back as if she were ravenous for him, pressing herself nearer, so that her breasts crushed into his chest, trapping his rampaging cock against the hard boning of her corset. He didn't know if it was lust that was making him dizzy with longing, if it was relief. Or if it was something about Madeline Chartrand that was innately and uniquely capable of making him desperate for her.

But whatever it was, it was potent.

And it was dangerous.

He broke the kiss again, stepping back, extricating himself from her.

"Forgive me, lass," he managed, his voice rough and ragged. "I didnae intend tae take advantage of ye. It was merely my emotions getting the better of me."

"Yes." She inhaled sharply, her shoulders rising and falling, her gaze flitting from his. "Of course that was what it was. And you must forgive me as well. It wasn't my intention to..." She waved a hand, her expression as befuddled as he felt.

This was new.

He took a deep breath himself, willing his cockstand to abate. Hoping his senses would return to him. And yet, nothing changed. He still longed to haul her back into his arms and kiss her breathless.

Or better yet, to take her in his arms and carry her all the way back to Sherborne Manor. To take her to his bedroom, lay her in his bed, and...

He shook his head.

What maggot had found its way into his brain? Clearly, his wits had been addled by those damned rocks. Perhaps he'd been hit by a falling stone and he hadn't realized it. Yes, that was the reason. He was likely concussed.

"Thank you," she said, still sounding breathless. "For saving me."

He flashed her a half grin, trying to calm his runaway ardor. "Think nothing of it, lassie."

"Oh dear." She frowned, catching her lower lip in her teeth and nibbling on it. "You're bleeding."

Aye, that explained it. Thank Christ.

"Where?" he asked, just as he felt a trickle of something warm and wet and decidedly not a raindrop rolling down his temple.

Instinctively, he raised a hand and wiped at it, examining his fingers to discover it was, in fact, blood. Now that he thought upon it, part of his head was aching something fierce, and he felt decidedly dizzier, curse it all.

Because Lachlan Macfie, present Duke of Kenross, rescuer of American heiresses, and proud Scot, was afraid of blood.

His vision went black around the edges.

And then, every blessed thing else went dark too, and the abyss claimed him.

CHAPTER 4

*L*achlan Macfie had kissed her, and then he had
swooned.

He'd kissed her well.

Kissed her too well.

Far too well.

And Madeline? She had liked it.

She frowned from her vigil at the window in her guest
bedchamber where she had retreated after she and Lachlan
had returned to the manor house. They'd been sodden, dirty,
and, in his case, bloodied. Back at the castle, he had dropped
like a tremendous tree being felled in a forest after he'd seen
the blood from the gash in his head. She had roused him,
cleaned his wound with a handkerchief, and together, they
had walked away from the castle ruins. They'd arrived to a
household in uproar, bedraggled and injured but alive.

"Something is bothering you," her sister, Lucy, said in that
knowing way she had, startling Madeline from her ruminations. "Were you hurt in the wall collapse after all?"

Madeline had been bustled off to her room, and Lachlan
had departed for his. A great, lumbering Scot who seemed

bemused and perhaps even a trifle concussed, holding a bloodied scrap of linen to his head.

He'd saved her.

Saved her with his big, powerful body, placing himself at great peril so that she would escape unscathed. And afterward, when they'd emerged from the collapsing castle to the daylight beyond, he had lowered his mouth to hers and taken her lips in a way no man before him ever had.

"He kissed me," she blurted, her eyes trained on the bucolic landscape beyond the rain-spattered windowpanes.

But he hadn't *just* kissed her. He had moved her. He had made her feel things. Unexpected things. Things she didn't want to feel, particularly in relation to a fortune-hunting Scotsman who wanted to marry her for her dowry.

Had she learned nothing from Charles? It would seem painfully apparent that she hadn't.

"He kissed you?" Lucy repeated.

Madeline sighed and turned away from the window to pin her sister with a glare. "Did I say that?"

Lucy's brows were arched, and she crossed her arms over her bodice in a defiant pose that suggested she wouldn't settle for anything less than a full confession. "I'm afraid you did."

"I should have kept it to myself," she grumbled.

Her sister grinned unrepentantly. "If you had, then I wouldn't be able to tease you about it."

Sisters. Madeline supposed it was only fair that Lucy tease her, for she couldn't lie. She'd certainly done more than her fair share of prodding Lucy about her midnight tryst with the Earl of Rexingham, whom she'd mistaken for a footman. The interlude had ultimately led to Lucy and Rexingham's engagement, much to her sister's dismay, as Lucy and Madeline had both been hoping to avoid their mother's matrimonial aspirations for them.

And now, it seemed as if they were about to find themselves trapped. Sooner rather than later for Lucy.

Madeline huffed a sigh. "Precisely."

"I might remind you that you were only too pleased to crow about my impending nuptials with Lord Rexingham," her sister said tartly.

"Of course I was." Madeline winced. "And now I'm paying the price, aren't I?"

"Well, you would be paying the price if you were marrying Mr. Macfie."

The memory of his mouth, hot and hungry and demanding, rose to taunt her.

"Thankfully, I'm not," she added hastily.

"Of course you aren't marrying him," Lucy said agreeably, giving her a sisterly look that said far more than her words had.

Madeline's eyes narrowed. "What?"

"You're flushing."

Her cheeks were annoyingly hot.

She fanned herself with her hand in absence of a proper implement. "It's warm in here."

"It's actually a bit chilly," Lucy countered.

The day had become cool after the rain and thunderstorms had passed through. But never mind that.

She seized at another excuse. "I took a very warm bath."

"If you say so, darling."

It was Madeline's turn to cross her arms. "What are you implying?"

"It is only that I know you, dear. I haven't seen you this flustered over a man since—"

"Don't say his name," Madeline interrupted, grimacing. "I prefer to call him Beelzebub."

Charles, that spawn of the devil. That devious, handsome

bastard. That soulless confidence man who had almost proven her ruin.

"Beelzebub, then," Lucy finished, her tone agreeable. "It's far too nice a name for him, you know."

"It is." Madeline sighed again, even more agitated than she'd been at her return to the house. Not because of those kisses or that brawny, too-handsome Scot, she told herself firmly. "Did I tell you that he's a duke?" she added before she could think twice about it.

"Beelzebub?" Lucky asked, wrinkling her nose. "I thought he was American. How can that be? Are you sure he isn't lying, dearest? You know that if he's speaking, chances are, it's a prevarication. Did he send you a letter, trying to win you back with more of his scheming lies?"

"Not Beelzebub. *Mr. Macfie*," she elaborated. "He's apparently just inherited a Scottish dukedom and a decrepit castle. He's looking for a wife. Don't tell Mother."

"I won't tell her. She'll be determined to see the two of you wed. She'd have the duke she's been vying for and an earl as well. It's her dream come to life." She paused, frowning. "How do you know Mr. Macfie is looking for a wife?"

"Because he asked me to marry him."

Lucy's eyes went wide. "Was this before or after he saved your life and kissed you?"

Madeline plucked at her skirts, frowning. "Before. Does it matter? I've told him I won't marry him, in no uncertain terms. He's looking for a marriage in name only, and I'm not looking for a marriage at all."

"But Mother and Father are pressing you to wed now that I've become betrothed to Rexingham," Lucy said, frowning thoughtfully.

The reminder of her conversation with their mother filled Madeline with apprehension. "I've been ordered to choose a husband before you marry the earl, or Father will select one for me."

"Good heavens, he intends to choose someone for you?" Lucy looked horrified at the prospect.

And Madeline knew why. Their father didn't pay much attention to anything that wasn't related to either his businesses or his money. He doled out his affections sparingly to his children, but there was no denying that their brother was his favorite child. Their father would do anything for his only son, who would one day inherit his empire. Lucy and Madeline, however, were relegated to the status of pawns. Their marriages were meant to complement their father's wealth and power. To achieve the ultimate social status their mother had longed for her entire life. She wanted to rule over not just elite New York society, but London as well.

"I hope he is blustering," Madeline said. "I can't truly believe Father would force me into marrying someone of his choosing."

"I can," Lucy said grimly. "Is allowing our father to select your husband a risk you want to take?"

Madeline shook her head, trying not to shudder at the prospect. "Allowing him to choose my future husband would be horrible. He would probably expect me to marry someone just like him."

Someone who buried himself in his own wealth and concerns. Someone who scarcely noticed she existed. No, she couldn't bear it. The future loomed before her, terrifyingly somber and unwanted. If she didn't want her father to choose a husband for her, however, she was going to have to do something about it. To find a potential husband of her own. And her time was already dwindling.

"You're going to have to choose someone yourself, my dear," Lucy said gently, echoing Madeline's own thoughts.

"Otherwise, you're consigning yourself to a lifetime of misery."

These were not the words Madeline wanted to hear from her sister, even if Lucy had reached the same conclusion Madeline had. Not now, particularly after those earth-shattering kisses she had shared with Lachlan Macfie. And not after that same man had proposed a cold, heartless union to her.

"I won't marry a man who only wants me for my fortune," she vowed firmly, for she had already suffered enough heartache at Charles's hands.

He had claimed to love her, only to later disclose his true motives. Thankfully, he'd done so before it had been too late and she had bound herself to him inextricably.

But then she thought again of the tall, rugged Scot who had spared her from being crushed beneath the castle wall. He couldn't be more different from Charles. First, he'd been open and honest about what he wanted from her. Second, he wasn't driven by greed; he had seemed concerned with the responsibilities weighing on him as the new duke. He'd mentioned the people depending upon him.

And his kisses...

"Maybe you should give Mr. Macfie a chance," Lucy urged. "You seem rather smitten with him."

"I'm not smitten," she denied instantly. "I'm merely... grateful to him for saving me."

"As you should be. Vivi said the weight of the castle wall would have decimated most men."

Yes, he was delightfully broad and tall, his body hewn of powerful muscle that she couldn't help to not only appreciate, but admire. To say nothing of his pleasantly deep voice that was rich as butter or his Scottish burr that never failed to have an effect upon her.

Lass.

She liked when he called her that.

Heaven help her, what was wrong with her?

"I'm not marrying Lachlan Macfie," she said, as much to herself as to her sister. "Or the Duke of...drat. I still can't recall his title."

"Ask him," Lucy urged her, giving her shoulder a gentle, sisterly pat of reassurance. "I think you should consider him, dearest. Grant him a chance. You may be surprised by what you find."

"As you did with the earl, you mean?" Madeline asked archly.

For they both knew that Lucy had done everything in her power to avoid marriage as well. In the end, it had been yet another clandestine tryst with Rexingham and the untimely arrival of the gossiping Lady Featherstone that had made the decision for her.

"My circumstances are different from yours," Lucy said, her frown returning. "My lack of discretion with the earl left me with no choice. I want better for you. I want you to be able to choose the husband you want for yourself, rather than to allow Mother and Father to browbeat you into a match that will make you miserable."

"Do you think you'll be miserable with the earl?" Madeline asked, searching her sister's gaze, wondering how the two of them had found themselves in this position so suddenly.

Two sisters determined not to marry. One destined to wed an earl in two months and the other forced into finding her future husband in that same amount of time.

"I hope we'll make each other happy," Lucy said, sighing heavily. "But it's you I'm most concerned about at the moment, dearest. The die has already been cast for me. I want you to find contentedness with someone who deserves you. I saw the way Mr. Macfie was looking at you earlier when the two of you returned. And seeing your reaction now...there's something between you. Don't tell me there isn't. I'm your sister, and I can read your face as if it were a book."

Madeline wanted to deny it. But then she thought about those kisses.

"You know it's true," Lucy pressed.

Madeline made an indelicate sound and moved back to the window, vexed with her sister for seeing so much.

For seeing *too* much.

"I don't think I even like the man," she murmured without conviction.

Lucy laughed. "Trust me, dearest. Liking a man doesn't necessarily have a thing to do with enjoying his kisses."

She slanted another glare in her sister's direction. "Who said I enjoyed them?"

"Your face did, darling."

Madeline surrendered to her inner childishness and stuck out her tongue at her sister. It was hardly an appropriate response, but in her current state, it was all she could manage.

Lucy laughed delightedly. "If I had a pie, I'd throw it at you."

Their food fights in the massive nursery of their Upper Fifth Avenue mansion were the stuff of legends. Until their mother had caught wind of their antics and put an end to all their fun.

"If I had an aspic, I'd toss it back," Madeline countered. "They looked the silliest when they sailed through the air before landing with the most satisfying splat."

"Poor Nurse." Lucy shook her head. "We were truly hellions, were we not?"

"We were dreadful children," Madeline agreed, thinking back on their childhood fondly.

She and Lucy had always been close. And suddenly, reality struck rather like the lightning that had hit the tree. When Lucy married the earl, she would be remaining here in England. If Madeline returned home to New York City with Mother, she'd find herself tied up in a loveless high-society marriage. She'd scarcely ever see Lucy.

"What is it, darling?" Lucy asked, her brow furrowed.

She was remarkably adept at understanding Madeline's thoughts. Sometimes before Madeline comprehended them herself.

A wave of melancholy washed over her. "When you marry Rexingham, you'll be staying here in England. But if I don't find a husband before the next two months are at an end, I'll be forced to go back home and marry someone of Father's choosing. We'll never see each other."

Lucy sobered as the undeniable truth of their circumstances settled upon her as well. "We can write each other letters."

"Letters!" Madeline shook her head, staving off a rush of tears. "Letters can never compare. I won't have anyone in New York City without you."

"You'll have Mother and Father and Duncan," Lucy offered, the tone of her voice suggesting she knew what a lackluster offering the three of them were.

Not that their brother wasn't a caring brother. He was, to the extent he was capable. Father had cast him in his own mold, and Duncan would be taking the reins of his empire one day, wearing his crown. Duncan knew it.

"They'll never hold a candle to you," Madeline said sadly. "There's no hope for it. I'm going to have to find a husband here in England. I'll marry him and stay here, and one day, our children can throw pies and creams at each other in the nursery, carrying on our family tradition."

Lucy's smile turned wistful. "That would be lovely, wouldn't it? I would adore it if you stayed here with me, dearest. The notion of marrying Rexingham and being left here without you is rather daunting, even with our coterie of friends."

"Our friends," Madeline echoed. "They need us. The Lady's Suffrage Society needs us."

"*I* need you, sister." Lucy reached for her hand, giving it a loving squeeze. "It's settled. You'll find a husband at once. Why not Mr. Macfie…er, the duke?"

Somehow, they'd come full circle and were back to *him*.

Lachlan Macfie.

Madeline recalled again the way he'd kissed her. The way she'd felt in his strong arms. So protected and secure. He was devilishly handsome. He'd been honest about his intentions. Which reminded her…

"He wants a marriage in name only, Luce," she said, reverting to the childhood nickname she'd had for her sister. "If I do wed, I think I'd like children."

"A marriage in name only? Not even Rexingham wants that. I'm to be his broodmare for his heir and spare." Lucy paused, frowning. "But Mr. Macfie kissed you, did he not? He couldn't be entirely frigid."

Oh, how he had.

Warmth crept over her cheeks. "It could have been an aberration. An instinctive reaction to the danger we'd just faced."

Lucy raised a brow. "There's only one way to be certain if it was."

"What's that?" Madeline asked, fearing she already knew the answer.

"Kiss him again," Lucy said matter-of-factly. "And then you'll know not just if it was an aberration but also if he's the man you want to marry."

∾

"Would you care to take a walk in the gardens?"

Lachlan blinked at Miss Madeline Chartrand, thinking he'd misheard her. Had the lass just invited him to accompany her somewhere? Mayhap that vicious knock he'd taken to the head was worse than he'd believed.

"A walk," he repeated as she stared up at him, her countenance bearing a pinched expression.

It was how he imagined she might look if she'd accidentally seated herself in a puddle.

"Yes." She smiled brightly, her cheer appearing forced. "A walk, Your Grace."

He looked around quickly to see if anyone had overheard. But everyone else in the great hall, coming and going from the breakfast room, was distracted by conversation or flitting to their next entertainment. The servants moved about with silent precision. No one was watching them.

"I havenae shared the news with most people just yet, lass," he told her quietly.

And he wasn't entirely sure why he hadn't. Years ago, he would have loved nothing better than to inherit a title and all the clout and power it would bring. Rose would have wanted him if he'd been the Duke of Kenross, and he had no doubt about it. But now, the title almost felt like a secret shame he wanted to keep hidden. He didn't feel like the Duke of Kenross. He felt like Lachlan Macfie, just as he'd always been and forever would be.

"Forgive me. I'd forgotten it was a secret," Miss Chartrand was saying. "What is the title again, if you please?"

"Kenross," he said grimly, not liking the way it sounded, the way it felt.

It didn't feel like him.

"Kenross," she repeated.

And damn him, but he *did* like the way it sounded in Miss Chartrand's crisp, clear American accent. In her sultry voice. Heat curled around him, and he found himself thinking about the way her lush lips had felt beneath his.

"Aye, that's me," he agreed grimly, banishing those unwanted musings. "And tae be certain, lass, ye wish tae take a walk in the gardens?"

"Yes."

"With me?"

She smiled, her eyes suddenly twinkling with suppressed mirth as some of the stiffness fled her posture. "Aye, with ye."

She was mimicking his Scots burr. And he liked that too. Far more than he would have expected.

"Ye might make a passable Scot yet, Miss Chartrand," he told her, keeping a teasing air.

Likely, she wanted to thank him for his efforts in the castle ruins the day before. Nothing more.

"Thank you." She eyed him searchingly, as if he possessed a secret she dearly longed to know. "Some fresh air would be just the thing, don't you think?"

The day beyond the windows was bright and cheerful. Nary a hint of rain.

"As long as we avoid castles, thunderstorms, and grizzly bears," he returned easily.

That earned him a chuckle and a true smile. God, she was breathtakingly lovely, Miss Madeline Chartrand. He wanted to kiss her again. But that was just the head that wasn't atop his shoulders thinking for him.

The lass refused ye, he reminded himself sternly.

Lachlan offered her his arm, and she took it. They stopped to retrieve hats and a wrap for her. And then, together, they moved through the great hall to the door that led to the sprawling Sherborne Manor park.

"I have it on good authority that England hasnae any

grizzly bears," she said as they rounded the path and approached the garden maze.

Her continued attempt at a Scottish accent was nothing short of adorable.

He had to tamp down a rising urge to tell her so and cleared his throat instead. "Aye, yer authority is a wise man."

"A wise and brave man." She cast a glance in his direction, her hat casting a shadow over her eyes, rendering their depths more mysterious. "A strong one as well. I'm not sure I thanked you properly for saving me yesterday."

"Yer safety is all the thanks I require, lass," he said.

If anything had happened to her yesterday—nay, it didn't bear contemplation. Miss Chartrand was here on his arm, the sun was shining overhead, and the day promised to be a glorious one. Even if he was a penniless duke without an inkling of how he would restore the estate he'd inherited and care for all the people who would be looking to him.

"If you hadn't chased after me when you did, and if you hadn't taken the brunt of that wall collapsing, I wouldn't be here," she said solemnly. "Thank you."

"Och." He scrubbed at his jaw, uncomfortable with her gratitude. "It's my fault ye went down that corridor. I did what anyone else would've done."

They proceeded along a straight portion of the boxwood maze, effectively swallowed by the large labyrinth, out of sight of their fellow houseguests. She kept up with his long-limbed strides with the same ease that she had before, and he found himself once again admiring her height. She was what his dear mother would have called a Long Meg. He hadn't realized that a woman's height would be so potent an aphrodisiac for him until this moment, this woman. Rose had been petite and fair-haired. Like a wee fairy.

But Madeline Chartrand was tall, gorgeous, chestnut-haired, and delectable. She had the sort of mouth a man couldn't look at without thinking about how it might look wrapped around his cock. Taking him deep.

Ah, damnation. He had to stop this utter madness where she was concerned. He didn't need to be lusting over her. He needed to find a wealthy wife and get his estate in order. But his vow to remain celibate had never been so tested.

"Not everyone would have saved me as you did," Miss Chartrand insisted, blithely unaware of his lewd thoughts. "Your size and your strength combined to make it possible. So I must thank you."

"If you must," he allowed, feeling heat creep up the back of his neck. He didn't deserve her praise. He was allowing his weak, base instinct to take control of him. "Just as I must apologize for what happened after we made our way out of the castle."

The kissing, he meant, unable to bring himself to say the words.

"I liked it," she said softly.

He drew to a halt, sure this time that he'd misconstrued what she'd said. "Lass?"

She faced him on the path, holding his gaze. "The kisses. I liked them."

He swallowed hard. "As did I, lass. Verra much."

More than he should have. More than he'd believed possible after all these years. After Rose had stolen his heart and then trampled on it, leaving him with nothing but his honor and his pride. Both had served him well. Until yesterday.

"I was wondering if we might try it again," Miss Chartrand said.

And Lachlan was so shocked that she could have knocked him onto his arse with nothing more than a feather.

"Try it," he repeated dumbly, even as his cock rose to attention, thickening and straining in his trousers.

"Try kissing," she elaborated, then caught her lower lip in her teeth as if she wasn't certain she should dare to say more.

"Ye want me tae kiss ye?" he asked, his voice husky and low with desire that was suddenly roaring inside him like a blazing fire.

"Yes. I do. That is, if you don't mind. I was thinking that perhaps... I suppose it doesn't matter. Maybe this was a terrible idea after all, and I should—"

"Lass," he interrupted her sudden stream of words.

She blinked. "Yes?"

"Hush."

His head dipped, and he took her mouth with his. Her lips were as soft and supple as he remembered. The angle was perfection. *She* was perfection. Sheer, womanly, decadent perfection.

His hands found her waist, drawing her nearer to him. How right it felt, the low sigh she made into his kiss, the way she melted into him, her curves pressing into his hardness, arms twining around his neck. She kissed him back, her lips responding to his with an ardor that made his cock go painfully rigid.

The sweet scent of flowers wrapped around him like Highlands mist. The scent of Miss Chartrand. *Madeline.* That was her given name. They were certainly beyond formality now. He groaned because he couldn't help himself. He was fast coming undone, and it was all her fault. He had to have another taste of the honeyed warmth of her mouth. She opened for him, her tongue tentatively meeting his.

And everything else ceased to exist.

The manor house presiding over them, their fellow guests, birds flying above and trilling from the trees, the sky and clouds, earth and heaven and hell. There was nothing but Lachlan and the firebrand in his arms. She made a throaty sound. The sound a lover made when she wanted more, her lips seeking his with more determined pressure. She was, he realized, every bit as ravenous for him as he was for her.

The discovery sent his restraint crashing down like the centuries-old castle wall that had threatened to bury them alive. But Lachlan didn't care. He had never been struck by such an urge—to claim, to take, to consume. To ravish her lips and leave his mark on her. Their mouths fused, their tongues glided in sinuous tandem, and their bodies wound together naturally, as if they had been made for this moment of passion in the garden maze.

It was unsettling, the potency of the effect she had on him. But he was helpless to do anything other than feed her kisses. To give her his tongue. To nip her full lower lip until she whimpered and then ease the sting with another kiss. Sweet like a ripened summer berry, that was what she was. Something to be savored. Lachlan's mouth left hers to rain a trail of kisses along the creamy smoothness of her jaw. He inhaled sharply, basking in the scent of woman and roses and lily of the valley. Like a garden in bloom.

A growl tore from him. He felt like a rampaging warrior on the battlefield, emerging victorious from amongst his fallen foes. He felt *alive*. His hands flexed on her waist, his fingers thwarted by the harsh boning of her corset and layers of silk and undergarments. He longed for bare skin, for curves, for softness.

The brim of her hat was in the way.

So was his.

He reached up, plucking first hers and then his away, not caring where they fell. Better. He kissed her temple, his lips grazing her skin, then her sleek chestnut hair, which had been pulled away from her lovely face and into an elaborate knot of sorts. His hand settled on the small of her back, that natural cove, aligning her more fully with him.

His body was roaring with need the likes of which he hadn't experienced in as long as he could recall. He *wanted*. God above, how he wanted. He was aflame with need, every part of him yearning to back her into the boxwood hedge behind them, grasp a handful of her skirts, and lift them to her waist. To reach beneath and find the slit in her drawers. To part her folds and see if she was wet for him.

He kissed her throat, openmouthed and desperate. It was as if some door inside him had burst open, and now he couldn't keep all the raging lust within from pouring forth. Even her skin tasted sweet. He ran his tongue along the sensitive cord, gratified when she shivered, her fingers digging into his shoulders as if she feared her knees would give way and she'd fall to the ground if she didn't hold tightly to him.

Suddenly, a bird called out as it passed low overhead, the sound jolting Lachlan back to the present abruptly. He lifted his head, setting Miss Chartrand away from him as if she were a venomous snake poised to strike. Because as dangerous as she was to him—to his sanity, his honor, his celibacy—she may as well have been. He didn't ravish women in gardens. He didn't kiss them until he was breathless and then contemplate lifting their skirts in the midst of a maze where anyone could happen upon them.

His eyes traveled over her, drinking her in. God. She was beautiful. Temptation incarnate, with her chestnut hair coming loose in wavy tendrils around her face, her lips swollen and painted cherry-red from his kisses. Her lashes low over her eyes, her breasts rising and falling with her ragged breaths. And the red blossoming on her throat from where he had kissed and sucked on her delicate skin.

He had done that. He was responsible for the way she looked, rumpled and delicious and overwhelmed by passion.

His heart was thundering in his chest, and lust was boiling through him like hot lava. He desired this woman.

Badly.

But then, as if they hadn't just shared a kiss that had singed him into a smoldering pile of ash, she smoothed her skirts calmly, her expression serene.

"That will do." She nodded as if she were at a shop, considering which pattern of fabric she ought to purchase.

For a moment, he struggled to find words. To find a damned language. His wits were beyond addled. Another deep breath, and sanity slowly began restoring itself.

"It will?" His brows crashed together. "What will do, lass?"

"The kisses." A smile curved her pretty lips. "*You* will do, in fact. I accept your proposal."

"Ye accept?" He was dumbfounded.

What was she talking about? Had he missed a vital part of their conversation thus far? Had her lips beneath his completely ravaged his memory?

She frowned, still smoothing away at the gathered fall of her skirt. "That is, if the offer is still available?"

The offer.

His proposal.

Understanding dawned. Miss Chartrand was speaking of his proposal of marriage. The one she had so summarily dismissed.

"My proposal, ye mean tae say?" he asked, his voice roughened with lust he still had yet to completely quell.

"Yes." She smiled, those full, well-kissed lips drawing his attention again. "Your proposal of marriage. You still need a wife with a fortune, do you not?"

She wanted to marry him? Perhaps she was the one who had taken a blow to the head yesterday and he'd failed to realize it. Christ, she was speaking as if it were a business proposal instead of an offering of marriage. But then, he hadn't been particularly romantic about it when he'd asked for her hand, had he?

"Aye," he managed. "I do still need a bride with a sizable dowry."

"Good." She nodded again. "It seems we're in agreement, then."

"We are?" Lachlan raked a hand through his thick hair, not caring if he left it standing on end.

He didn't think he'd ever been more bemused or befuddled, all at once.

"I find myself in need of a husband after all," she explained. "And I have a fortune. You require a wife who has a fortune. Your kisses are agreeable to me. I needed to be certain, given the possibility you might change your mind about the marriage being in name only."

"I willnae change my mind," he denied swiftly, even as his body suggested otherwise.

The desire flooding his veins and pulsing in his cock said he would have changed his mind right there in the maze, making a liar of him.

"Oh," she said, looking taken aback. Perhaps even insulted. "I suppose that's just as well."

"Why, lass?" He eyed her suspiciously, his masculine pride smarting. "Did ye no' like the kiss? I thought ye said it would do."

"I liked it too much," she said earnestly.

Her admission hit him in the chest with the force of a blow. Because he felt the same way. Some part of him instantly, instinctively knew that he should find a different woman for the role because this one was dangerously capable of causing him pain. And he couldn't help but think that surely there would be an heiress out there who wouldn't nearly bring him to his knees with a few mere kisses, that he should find her and beg her to become his bride instead.

But he didn't do that.

Because he was running out of time. Because he had the weight of an estate and all its people on his shoulders. Because kissing Madeline Chartrand had been the best damned thing to happen to him in what felt like forever.

And because he wanted to kiss her again.

This was a bad idea. A terrible, horrible, no-good idea. He was going to do it anyway.

"Ye'll marry me, then?" he asked stupidly.

Her smile faded, and he mourned its loss. "I will, Your Grace."

"Call me Lachlan," he said gruffly, disliking the formality and reminder of his unwanted title more than he could convey.

"Lachlan," she repeated, and then she held her hand out for him.

Lachlan accepted her hand, and she gave it a firm shake. What a peculiar woman she was. He felt as if he'd just made a deal with the devil.

CHAPTER 5

*M*adeline was getting married.

To the red-haired Scottish giant who had trampled her train and spilled champagne on her. To a man whose kisses made her toes curl in her fashionable boots even though he wanted a marriage in name only.

But most importantly of all—to Mother, at least—to a man who was a duke.

Madeline might as well have announced she was engaged to the Prince of Wales for all the joy her mother emitted when she heard the news. She had squealed as if she'd seen a mouse.

"Two weddings?" Mother fanned herself now, beaming. "I'm to plan two weddings! Oh, my heart. I can scarcely believe my good fortune."

Damn and blast. That wasn't what Madeline wanted.

"I don't think you'll need to plan mine," Madeline hastened to tell her, frowning. "I believe we'll be married quietly. And quickly."

Because that was what she wanted. The very notion of Mother forcing her to go to Paris to be fitted for a gown or making her listen to endless sermons about the types of flowers that ought to be used to decorate the church made Madeline want to hide. To run. To disappear.

She shuddered. Poor Lucy could bear the brunt of Mother's machinations. The Earl of Rexingham had decreed the wedding would be in two months' time, and he'd given Mother carte blanche. It was a dangerous mistake on the earl's part. But he would discover that soon enough on his own.

"Quickly?" Mother's face fell, her lip curling as if she'd scented something spoiled. "What do you mean quickly? Did something untoward occur between the two of you?"

The question wasn't unexpected. After all, Madeline and Lachlan had been alone together on more than one occasion.

"Of course nothing untoward occurred," she reassured her mother, heat sliding through her as she recalled those sinful kisses at the castle ruins.

Well, there had been that.

And then the kisses in the gardens also.

For such a massive man, Lachlan Macfie possessed a surprising amount of gentleness. And prowess. The man knew how to kiss. What else did he know? Part of her yearned to learn, even as she knew he had no intention of showing her. Why did the notion, which should have been freeing, suddenly seem so frustrating to her?

"Then I fail to see the reason for haste," Mother was saying, her tone one of vast displeasure. "Your wedding can follow Lucy's, my dear."

"No, it can't," she blurted, for now that she'd made her decision, she didn't want to wait. "His Grace has made it clear that he wishes for the wedding to be sooner rather than later."

Calling Lachlan *His Grace* felt odd. And not just because she'd been thinking of him as Mr. Macfie since the house party's beginning. But because she felt as if she knew him intimately now. His tongue had been in her mouth. Formality felt wrong.

"The duke can be patient. Goodness, one would think that he would want a bit of time to grow accustomed to his change of circumstance before rushing into marriage." Mother clucked her tongue, frowning peevishly, her disapproval evident.

This evening, when Madeline and Lachlan had announced their plans to marry, they had also informed all the guests in attendance that Lachlan was the new Duke of Kenross. Madeline had warned him privately that it would be necessary to make his title known. Otherwise, Mother and Father would never accept the proposal. Just as she had predicted, her mother had been overjoyed at the prospect of her daughter wedding a duke.

But being Mother, she couldn't simply accept that Madeline would become a duchess and that she had Lucy's wedding to the earl to plan. No, she had to insist upon a second *wedding of the century*, as she called it, to rival the first she was already eagerly orchestrating for Lucy.

"We aren't rushing into marriage," Madeline denied, even though the opposite was true. "Besides, you and Father impressed upon me how very important it was that I find a husband before Lucy's marriage to Rexingham. I've done what you asked. One would think you'd be pleased."

"I *am* pleased." Mother patted her arm absently, her countenance suggesting that her mind was whirling with a myriad of subjects that didn't pertain to Madeline. "A duke and an earl for my daughters—it's a feather in my cap. But these things must be done properly, my dear."

By properly, her mother meant spending a small fortune on silk, flowers, diamonds, and whatever else she deemed necessary for the wedding of the century.

Things Madeline didn't want or need.

"No," she said firmly.

Her mother blinked as if the word were foreign to her. Indeed, it likely was. No one denied Mrs. William Chartrand whatever whim she wished for in the moment.

"What do you mean, dearest?"

"I mean that I don't want a wedding like the one you're planning for Lucy," she elaborated. "I want a wedding that is small and private. I don't want to wait over two months for it to be done. I want it to happen as quickly as possible."

In short, she wanted the business of the ceremony itself to be over. She wanted to be free of her mother and father's reign. She wanted the independence Lachlan had dangled so temptingly before her. The freedom she'd been too stubborn to see when she had refused him. It had taken her father's august ultimatum, coupled with Lucy's sage advice, to make Madeline realize marrying Lachlan would grant her the future she wanted for herself.

Well, aside from the moldering castle in Scotland.

She could do without ever having to see castle ruins again after her scare here in Yorkshire. Her throat still went tight with remembered terror at the memory of the stones closing in on her and Lachlan.

Her mother's lips tightened into a severe line. "I don't like the sound of this, Madeline. You've always been the dutiful daughter. Lucy has been my wayward child, and now it is you who seeks to defy me, on the eve of everything I've ever wanted finally being within my grasp."

And there was the truth of it, laid out without artifice.

Mother was only concerned with what *she* wanted. Not with what her daughters hoped for. Their desires for their own futures were entirely immaterial in comparison to the gloating rights Mother hoped to obtain over her fellow socialites in New York City.

"I'm still a dutiful daughter," she told her mother, trying to tamp down the sadness that rose inside her whenever she thought of how little Mother truly knew her. "I'm merely a daughter who doesn't wish for all the pomp and circumstance you want in my wedding. Should I not have a say in the matter?"

"Well, of course you should, dearest. However, your father will demand a ceremony befitting your place in society."

How like Mother to blame this on Father. He had his own sins to answer for, and he was every bit as concerned with his standing, wealth, and power. However, Madeline had no doubt that it wasn't Father who demanded a massive display for his daughters' weddings. That was all her mother's doing.

"I'm marrying the duke as soon as I'm able," she insisted, refusing to budge from her position. "We'll have the banns read and marry in three weeks."

"Three weeks?" Mother fanned herself wildly, looking as if she was going to swoon. "That's not nearly enough time."

"It's going to have to be," Madeline said. "It's what the duke wants."

"It is?"

She saw her mother softening, relenting. Putting Lachlan's wishes first, and merely because he was the Duke of Kenross. Try as she might not to allow that to hurt her, Madeline's heart gave a pang.

"Yes, it is," she confirmed, and not without a hint of bitterness seeping into her voice. "I'm afraid we have no choice but to honor His Grace's wishes."

A peculiar mixture of relief and trepidation swept over Madeline, her shoulders sagging. She hadn't even realized she'd been holding herself stiffly until this moment, her mother's reluctant capitulation chasing her fear that she would find herself wrapped up in a spectacle of a wedding.

It was settled.

She was going to marry Lachlan Macfie and become the next Duchess of Kenross.

What had she done?

~

LACHLAN STUDIED THE LOVELY, determined woman who was soon going to be his wife, wondering what the devil he'd been thinking to propose to someone so beautiful.

So tempting.

So dangerous.

Someone who had stolen into his bedchamber and awaited him when he returned from port and cigars with the gentlemen of the house party. And there had been a great deal of port consumed in honor of his impending nuptials. So much that he was feeling a wee bit soused. And that was why he was certain he'd misunderstood when she'd announced that she had told her mother they'd be marrying in three weeks' time.

"Ye told yer mother what, lass?" he asked, trying not to take note of how near she stood to his bed.

Nor the way her pink silk evening gown clung to her curves in all the right ways.

"That we're marrying as soon as possible." She bit her lip, looking hesitant then and infinitely kissable. "I hope you don't mind. It was the only conceivable way to extricate ourselves from her wedding plans."

He shouldn't be thinking about kissing Madeline Chartrand, he reminded himself sharply. Shouldn't be looking at her soft, lush lips. But his mind was somehow indistinct at the moment, thanks to all that damned port.

"Yer mother had wedding plans?" His brows rose. "Already?"

They'd only just announced their engagement that evening. He was still growing accustomed to the notion he would be marrying someone—anyone—and most particularly someone who wasn't Rose. The entire process had somehow seemed far easier when it had been a notion in his mind.

"My mother has likely been planning my wedding ever since I was a debutante," Madeline said, her tone one of resignation. "I'm afraid she can be quite impossible when she wishes."

"Impossible would be one word for it, lass," he said, rubbing his jaw.

He had spoken with Mrs. Chartrand directly after his discussion in the garden earlier with Madeline. He had also sent a telegram to her father, officially asking permission to wed his daughter. The man's response had been sparse but favorable. Lachlan hadn't been able to shake the suspicion that both Mr. and Mrs. Chartrand cared a great deal more about who their daughter would be marrying than whether he would prove a good husband or make her happy.

As it happened, Lachlan wasn't so certain he was capable of the latter. But he would try. Madeline deserved that much.

"She is overzealous," Madeline agreed, sighing heavily. "So, you see, it really is necessary for us to have the banns called and marry with all haste. If we tarry, she'll only start demanding I accompany her and Lucy to Paris for a gown fitting."

"Ye dinnae want tae go tae Paris for a gown?"

It occurred to him then that most ladies of his acquaintance would adore the chance. And in short order, it also occurred to him that he scarcely knew anything about the woman who would become his bride, aside from how good she felt in his arms and how delectable her lips were.

"Of course not." Madeline was frowning at him, as if he

had suggested she ought to saddle a horse and ride to the moon. "It would be torturous being there with Mother. I doubt poor Lucy will ever recover from the horrors of it. It's almost certain that Mother will choose every detail for her. She'll likely walk down the aisle looking like she was in a battle with a rose garden and lost."

Poor Lucy Chartrand, indeed. Lachlan was beginning to hope his future bride wasn't anything like her termagant mother.

"We cannae have that," he agreed. "But let's discuss something of even greater import than the timing of our wedding, shall we, lass? Such as what are ye doing stealing about Sherborne Manor and hiding in my bedroom? Surely ye ken ye ought no' tae be here."

"I needed to speak with you," she said simply. "It seemed the most expedient fashion of having a moment alone, particularly since you joined the gentlemen following dinner and I was left to my mother's haranguing."

He winced. "But it's wrong, lass. If anyone were tae discover ye here..."

"We'd have to marry," she finished, smiling at him in a way that made his cock twitch to attention. "And since we're already doing that, it shouldn't matter. We're nearly husband and wife already."

Lachlan shook his head, feeling dizzy, and not from the port. "Ye only agreed tae marry me this afternoon. And yer father just sent a telegram with his blessing before dinner."

He should have chosen a nice, shy, biddable lass. One like Lady Edith Smythe. Not this American hellion.

"There's nothing untoward about my being here," she said, moving toward him. "It's hardly as if you would be overwhelmed by lust in my presence. You want a chaste marriage. We'll be friends."

Ah, blast. She was still coming closer, cutting away the

safe distance between them that had rendered it impossible for him to touch her. The scent of rose and lily of the valley hit him. And the lust she had just breezily assumed he didn't possess was roaring and raging through his blood.

He held up a hand. "Stop there, where ye are. Dinnae come any closer, lass."

"Why?" She stopped, miraculously obeying him, her brows drawn together.

"Because if ye come any closer, I'll be tempted tae do something I shouldnae."

Like touch her. Take her in his arms. Kiss her again.

More than that.

Och, what had he been thinking, choosing this woman as his future bride? Aye, he needed her dowry, but how was he to resist her and keep his vow to himself? And it was an important vow, damn it.

He had no wish to ever make himself vulnerable again. Not after what he'd endured with Rose. He owed it to himself to make certain that he would never be so weakened by a woman. Lachlan moved himself subtly, positioning his body—and his rampaging cock—behind a wingback chair.

"Tempted to do what?" Madeline wanted to know.

Of course she did. The lass was far too curious and bold.

"Tae kiss ye again," he ground out grimly. "And that willnae do."

"Why not? I liked your kisses."

Lust shot through him. He gripped the back of the chair to keep from reaching for her. "Ye shouldnae say such things tae a man, lassie."

He'd liked her kisses as well. Liked her lush mouth, her tongue gliding against his in sinuous rhythm.

Her unusual gaze studied him, dropping to the chair and then traveling back to meet his. "Are you hiding behind the chair?"

"I'm no' hiding," he grumbled.

But he *was* using the piece of furniture as a shield. This way, he couldn't walk toward her, and she also couldn't see the effect she was having on him, which was unfortunately obvious, given that Lachlan was a large man—*everywhere*.

"You don't trust yourself not to kiss me," she guessed wisely. "Is that it?"

"Of course I trust myself." He trusted the head on his shoulders anyway. He'd been able to keep himself out of scrapes for years by burying himself in business and making sure he was so busy that there'd been neither time nor inclination for anything romantic in nature.

But clearly, he hadn't thought his plan through when he had settled upon wedding the lovely woman who had invaded his bedchamber without a second thought. Was she a witch, to have cast a spell over his poor cock? Aye, mayhap. Lachlan narrowed his eyes at her, considering.

"Then why are you gripping the chair as if it might protect you from me?"

Madeline Chartrand was grinning at him, and by the rood, she wore amusement the way some women wore a fine silk. When she smiled, she looked nothing short of lusciously fuckable, and that was a problem.

A massive problem.

He cleared his throat, chasing the desire clogging it. "Because I'm trying tae keep yer reputation in mind, lass. Ye cannae go clanging about a man's bedchamber like this."

"I don't recall making much noise." She was moving again.

Coming nearer. Skirting the chair, and damn his eyes for settling on the way her bodice clung lovingly to her breasts. Because now he couldn't breathe.

"Lachlan?" She laid a hand on his sleeve, searing him through his tweed coat.

He was reasonably certain he might snap the chair in two like a twig.

"Ye cannae be here," he said sternly, clinging to his sense of honor.

To the moral code that had never failed him once. Not in all the years since he'd left Scotland and Rose behind.

"Are you angry with me?"

"I'm angry with myself," he admitted.

Because he couldn't seem to keep from wanting her. And that was a very bad, impossible thing, his wanting her. Desire inevitably led to tender feelings, and tender feelings led to pain, and he'd had enough pain to last a lifetime.

"Because you want to kiss me?" she guessed, her lips tipping upward in seductive invitation.

That was all it required. Her sly question. Her smile. Her hand on his sleeve. Something inside Lachlan snapped. Perhaps it was his tenuous hold on his restraint. Perhaps it was the last remaining thread of his sanity. Whatever it was, it had broken him.

He watched himself moving as if in a dream. His hands released their hold on the chair and reached for her, settling on her waist. One swift motion, and he pulled her against him, her body molding to his and setting him aflame. She was so soft. Everywhere. He'd forgotten how good it felt to hold a woman.

Madeline had reminded him. Worse, she had awakened him to the sheer joy of it. Of *her*. And that was more dangerous than any other realization, because this woman was going to be within reach. She was going to be his bloody wife.

Madeline wound her arms around his neck, and she pressed her breasts into his chest, a bountiful offering he couldn't refuse. Even with the layer of her corset and gown separating them, her softness felt so good, so right crushed into his hardness. Her curves were lush and full and womanly. He inhaled deeply, the scent of her invading his lungs, his nose, his head.

His wits were instantly scrambled. All the reasons that he should retreat from the room without touching her vanished from his mind. There was only the driving need to feel her against him. To kiss her breathless and senseless.

He lowered his lips to hers and claimed them, gathering her into him, reveling in her curves, in the soft sound she made in her throat, part sigh, part needy moan. As if she'd been waiting for this moment, for his kiss. Her tongue was there, eager and hot, demanding entry to his mouth.

He surrendered, giving her what she wanted with a groan of his own. She tasted like sweet wine and dessert, and he wanted to feast on her mouth. Wanted to peel her out of her gown and worship her everywhere. Wanted to forget why he should maintain a proper distance between them. Why decorum wasn't just wise but necessary.

Vital, even.

But nothing seemed more vital than her mouth sweetly coaxing a response from him, those full lips chasing his, demanding more of him than he was willing to give. He hadn't expected to admire her. To want her as he did. To be so consumed with desire that he lost control of the vow he'd made to himself when Rose had nearly decimated him and he'd left Scotland with the tattered remnants of his heart.

Madeline's kisses were decadent. Her lips were velvety and sleek and hot. But knowing. She was bringing him steadily to his knees.

This wasn't good.

He had to stop this madness.

Lachlan lifted his head with great reluctance. "Lass, we cannae carry on like this. It isnae fair to ye."

"It's only kissing. I haven't asked you to bed me."

The word *bed* on her berry-red lips. Lord above. All the saints and angels. He could scarcely think past the lust rushing through his blood.

"Ye do speak plainly," he managed, trying to cling to his determination to play the gentleman and keep his vow to himself. "Is that an American custom?"

"Perhaps it is. I've never thought about it." Madeline's gaze dipped to his mouth. "Why should we bother to speak any other way?"

Och, when she phrased it thus, how was he to argue? She made it sound so reasonable.

"I thought ye were a snob when I first met ye, but now I can see that I was wrong. Yer plain speech is refreshing, I'll grant ye that much. I like no' having to think in riddles and rhymes."

She laughed. "Is that a compliment or an insult? I confess, I can't quite be certain."

His ears went hot. Lachlan wasn't accustomed to flirting. Or impressing a woman. He'd spent years avoiding romantic entanglements. Burying himself in work and suppressing all his base needs.

"A compliment, lass," he managed hoarsely.

"I was merely unimpressed by what you did to my poor train." Holding his gaze, she reached for his face, lightly trailing her fingertips along his jaw in a caress that lit him up inside like electric lights. "What do you think of me now?"

"I think..." He paused, considering his words with great care as she nearly unmanned him by tracing the perimeter of his bottom lip with her forefinger. "I think ye're dangerous, lassie."

"Dangerous?" She settled her finger in the dip above his mouth. "In what way?"

"Dangerous to my determination."

He swallowed hard. Her finger had paused at his

philtrum, lingering there. He wanted to feel that finger investigating every part of him, from his mouth to his cock. Especially his cock. But then, she might use her whole hand for the purpose, along with her mouth...

"And what are you so determined to do, Lachlan?" she asked, her voice husky, her finger still laid there in that place he had never particularly concerned himself with until now.

Because now, it felt as if it were the most erotic place on his cursed body. It felt as if he might come just from her stroking him there.

"Assume my duties," he answered with great difficulty, his lips grazing the fleshy pad of her finger as he spoke. "Uphold the vow I've made tae myself. Restore the castle. Help the people dependent upon me. Marry ye."

"What is the vow you made to yourself?"

"I dinnae wish tae speak of it now," he protested.

"Tell me, if you please. I'm to be your wife. I should know these things."

"Ye neednae."

"I do need."

Her other hand was at his nape, toying with the strands of hair that he'd always worn too long to be fashionable. And God, but he loved the play of her fingers gently sifting and teasing his neck. Light grazes, scarcely anything at all, and yet she was driving him beyond the point of reason with these small suggestions of touch. Of the promise that awaited him if he only forfeited.

"Fine, then," he forced out. "My vow of celibacy, if ye must ken."

"Celibacy," she repeated, cocking her head.

Looking dazed.

Sounding confused.

And still touching him. Still making him mad with wanting her.

"Aye. It is when a man decides tae keep his doodle in his trousers where it belongs."

"Doodle?"

This wasn't going well.

"What do ye call a man's rod in America?" he asked stiffly, wishing his would wilt and cease pressing madly against his trousers. "A long fellow? A shaft of delight?"

Speaking about his, even in vagaries, was having a most undesired effect. If he didn't take care, he'd draw her into his arms, lay her down on the bed, and proceed to show her what he meant rather than explain with words.

She chuckled. "You certainly do have a vast vocabulary for describing a single appendage."

"It's arguably the most important one on a man, lass."

Madeline bit her lip. "I know what celibacy is, of course. What I was wondering is why you might have made such a vow, particularly since you're now taking a wife."

There was one reason in particular, but he didn't wish to speak of that. Or think about it. It felt disastrously wrong with the beautiful, vibrant woman he was going to marry invading his space. Looking up at him with inquisitive dark gray eyes, her mouth swollen from his kisses.

"Ye neednae concern yerself with the reason," he said.

"Do you have a venereal disease?" She wanted to know.

Lachlan nearly swallowed his tongue.

"Och, lass! Of course I dinnae have one. I've been living the life of a damned monk for years."

"Is there something...wrong with your...doodle?" she asked next, peering down at his trousers.

Where one could reasonably assume she'd have a view of the fine form his prick was currently in.

"Madeline," he said in strangled protest.

"If we're to be married, I ought to know," she said reasonably. "As your wife, I'll need to understand the reasoning behind your vow, even if the subject is a rather delicate one."

This woman. She was going to be the death of him. He'd either expire from rampaging lust or from embarrassment before they were even wed. He was sure of it.

"See here, lass," he growled. "There isnae anything delicate about my cock."

To give proof, he took her hand in his and pressed it to where his demanding prick was currently pressing rigidly against the tweed. Her eyes went wide, her lips parting. And the second she stroked him, he had to set his molars on edge to keep from spending in his trousers like a stripling.

Providing evidence of his hale and hearty constitution had clearly been a mistake. A prideful, colossally stupid mistake. Because now her hand was on him. Investigating. And dear saints, he thought he might die from the pleasure of it.

"Oh my," she said. "You're right. Not delicate at all."

She stroked him again, traveling from root to tip, and he didn't know if he'd somehow stumbled into the practiced hands of a seductress, if she was allowing her instinct to guide her, or if his body was simply like a primed pump, ready to surrender at the slightest touch.

"Ye shouldnae be touching me thus," he managed to say, feeling light-headed.

Because he wanted her to touch him this way. He wanted her to open the fall of his trousers and take him in hand. He wanted those berry lips to close around the tip, and he wanted her to suck him down her throat.

No, no, no.

Wrong, wrong, wrong.

"Do you not like it?" She paused in her ministrations but didn't remove her hand, frowning. "In the books I've read, when a lady touches a man's cock, he feels great pleasure."

Lachlan couldn't manage a word. Nothing but a half growl, feral and low.

And then he forced himself to say something intelligible. A response. Honest but painful.

"I like it, lass. I like it too much."

"I like it too," she said.

Sweet saints. Heavens and all the angels.

Her fingers were working on the buttons fastening his trousers. And he was helpless to stop her. Because he thought he might die if she didn't touch his bare cock.

The breath fled him. His cock sprang free of his smalls. Massive and rude, just like the rest of him.

But she wrapped her hand around him, her touch tentative and soft, and then she stroked again. He was already leaking, and if she touched him for much longer, he was going to spend in her hand. At the moment, he wasn't sure he cared. Indeed, he wasn't sure of anything, including his own name.

"I like the way you feel," she said softly. "Your skin is so hot and smooth."

Fuck. He tried to think. Failed.

"I cannae... Lass, ye shouldnae..."

"Does it bring you pleasure?" She wetted her lips, looking roused herself.

The sight of Madeline stroking his bare cock, the both of them fully clothed, was the most erotic thing he'd ever beheld.

"Aye," he bit out.

"Tell me what to do."

What he should tell her to do was stop. He should tuck himself back into his trousers and recall the vow he'd made to himself. He ought to remember what it meant to be a gentleman.

But he was under this woman's spell now. And he wanted —he needed—more.

"Stroke me," he said. "Grip me harder."

His hand closed over hers, and he showed her what he liked, what he needed.

"Does that feel good?" she asked, her voice throaty.

The sorceress. The beautiful, cunning, delectable woman. She'd bewitched him. There was no other answer for what was happening. For what he was allowing to happen.

"Aye," he managed again as they both worked his cock in unison.

"Sometimes in the books I've read, the woman takes the man into her mouth."

Oh dear God. He thought about her lips and tongue on him. Thought about sliding into the velvety, sleek heat of her mouth. Thought about watching his thick cock disappear into those heavenly depths. And he couldn't hold back. He couldn't do anything but surrender.

"Fuck." His orgasm was fast and furious, rushing through him.

Pleasure burst inside him, like a dam had broken. It was strong and potent, stealing his breath, making his knees shake, sending black stars to dance across his vision. And still, she didn't stop, her firm grip on his cock making him lose control utterly.

Lachlan didn't even have the time to find a handkerchief to catch his spend. He spurted creamy white lashings all over her pink silk gown.

CHAPTER 6

$\mathcal{M}$adeline had never seen anything like what had just happened between herself and Lachlan. Objectively, she was sure she ought to be horrified at the lines of thick white marring her fine silk. But she couldn't summon a hint of outrage. All she felt was empowered.

She'd read about such things, of course. The books called it a man's spend. His seed. An emission. But those words provided pale descriptors.

She was flushed. Aching. Touching him had left her in a strangely wild state she'd never felt before. Pleasuring him had made her feel wanton and bold. This big man, her hulking Scot, utterly in her thrall.

She felt as if she had drunk too much wine. Inebriated on pleasure. As if she were teetering on the razor's edge of something glorious herself.

"Lass," Lachlan said, his voice thick and deep.

Almost tender.

She had released him after he'd spent, and now he tucked his cock back into his trousers hastily.

"We shouldnae have done that," he added.

"Did you like it?" she asked.

"Verra much." He sounded grim. "Can ye doubt it? I believe ye're wearing the evidence on yer skirts."

And to think she'd been furious over the champagne he'd spilled on her train before.

She chuckled. "Do you have a handkerchief?"

"Och," he muttered, his cheekbones going red as he fumbled inside his coat, his large hand emerging victorious, a scrap of linen clutched in his long fingers. "Allow me tae clean the mess I've made. It would seem I'm destined tae ruin yer silk."

"I didn't mind as much this time," she told him honestly, holding still as he used the *mouchoir* to remove the streaks he'd left on her gown.

"I'll buy ye a new gown. Two new gowns." He wrinkled his nose. "I do have some funds of my own. Just not the vast sum required tae restore Castle Kenross."

For some reason, his offer touched her.

"You needn't worry about it," she reassured him. "Though, given the indiscretion that produced this particular stain, I likely won't consult my lady's maid about the best means of removing it."

He made a choked sound, finishing his task and striding to the fireplace to toss the besmirched handkerchief into the low embers as if he were burning the evidence of a crime. "There we are." He turned to a pitcher and bowl on a nearby stand and cleaned his hands, his broad back to her.

Was he embarrassed, she wondered?

Displeased with her for her forwardness? After all, he had mentioned a vow of celibacy. Did that mean he was stiff and proper? Was his vow going to extend to their marriage, or was he intending to remain chaste only until their wedding day?

Questions swirled. He had asked for a marriage in name

only, and he'd been quite firm on it. But Madeline knew now that she wanted more than that. More from Lachlan, specifically.

He finished washing his hands, dried them, and turned back to her. His expression was storm-tossed.

"Forgive me, lass. That was unaccountably rude. I shouldnae have allowed that tae happen."

Allowed it? As if she'd had no part in it? As if she hadn't wanted it every bit as much as he had? Madeline didn't like the guilt in his expression. She didn't like the regret either.

"You needn't apologize," she said firmly. "I enjoyed it."

"Ye..." His brow furrowed as his words trailed off, his befuddlement quite endearing. "Ye liked it?"

"Yes. And I'd like to do it again." She kept her tone matter-of-fact. "Only next time, I might prefer to use my mouth."

He stared at her, his gaze searing. "Ye're trying tae kill me. Is that it? Ye hate me, and ye've decided tae punish me before the felling blow."

What an odd man he was. One would think he would be overjoyed that she wanted his attentions. That she wanted to bestow hers upon him. In the books, there was a great deal of mutual enjoyment. And sometimes exclamations and creamy emissions.

"In the stories I've read, the gentlemen always enjoy it a great deal. I think you might as well."

His cheekbones went red again, rivaling his hair. "What manner of stories are ye reading?"

"The interesting kind, clearly." She moved to join him at the washstand, thinking him terribly handsome.

His tremendous size and strength were intriguing to her. She liked the notion that he could pick her up in his arms and carry her away. She liked that he had saved her from being crushed in the castle ruins. That he kissed her so sweetly. That he could be so bold and yet equally bashful, that he was tall and muscled and powerful and yet tender.

"I should... It isnae right that I enjoyed such pleasure and gave ye none." His gaze searched hers. "I should return the favor."

"Do you mean you want to touch me as well?" she asked, the notion sending fire through her blood.

"More than I want my next breath, lass. And that isnae what I want tae be feeling at the moment. Ye scare me."

That had her smiling. "I scare *you*? Judging by the size of your arms, I think it's safe to say you could beat me in a fair fight."

"What of an unfair one?" His tone was teasing, but his eyes had slipped to her lips.

She pretended to contemplate his question for an overly long moment, tapping her chin thoughtfully with her forefinger. "Who would be cheating, me or you?"

He passed his hand over his chin in a gesture she'd already come to recognize. "Ye, of course. How else would ye have a chance of winning?"

"Then I'd win," she said without hesitation.

His lips cocked up into a grin. "Sure of yerself, aye?"

"How should I be anything less? You've just shown you don't have the power to resist me. If the fight wasn't fair, I'd kiss you and unbutton your trousers, and you'd forget you were meant to be competing against me."

"Are ye a witch?"

His question made her blink. She certainly hadn't expected that.

Madeline frowned. "Of course not. I'm an American."

"I'm beginning to think that means ye are," he grumbled. "Because I find myself wanting tae kiss ye again and tae do things I shouldnae do."

His hands were at his sides, so strong and large, flexing as if he were tempted to reach for her. She wondered what they would feel like on the tender skin of her legs, her inner thighs. In her most intimate place. She wondered if she would like it if he touched her there. Madeline had a feeling she would, if the descriptions she'd read were at all accurate. She already knew she liked her own touch quite well.

"Who says you shouldn't?" she teased him lightly.

He was so stiff and rigid, his posture as stern as his voice, and she wondered what had happened to him to make him so distrustful of her. For surely that was the reason for his reaction. She couldn't think it anything else.

"My honor," he said.

"Honor is an admirable thing," she agreed, reaching for him bravely. She settled a hand on his hard chest, just over his madly thumping heart. "But I find myself curious, Lachlan."

"Curious?" he rasped, taking her wrist in a firm grip.

He was a big man, so very strong. But she felt utterly safe with him. Content in his presence, in his room. More so in his arms.

"Yes, curious," she repeated, elaborating on the profusion of feeling within her, some of which was even difficult to understand herself. "I've been reading bawdy stories for a long time, you see."

"God help me," he muttered.

"And it's made me wonder if everything I've read is true. If the sensations, the emotions, the mechanics of lovemaking are accurately depicted. I always imagined I'd take a lover one day since I never intended to marry. Maybe two."

He made a low, growling sound that rumbled in his chest.

"Or three," she continued, unable to resist prodding him for a reaction. "But since I'm going to have a husband, I can conduct the research myself."

"I was right. Ye're going tae be the death of me."

The soft burr of his accent wrapped around her, and he gently stroked the sensitive skin of her inner wrist with his thumb. His scent of soap and fir made her want to burrow her face into his broad chest and inhale deeply. Marrying this man wouldn't be a hardship at all. She only needed to persuade him that he didn't want a marriage in name only. And that his vow to himself was best forgotten.

"Will you kiss me again?" she asked.

"Lass."

He groaned. But before she could say another word, his head dipped and he sealed his mouth over hers. The kiss was ravenous, making a liar of the stoic face he had presented in the wake of his earlier passion. He had spoken of bringing her pleasure. She knew he could do so without making love to her. Perhaps they could skirt his vow to himself. She wasn't too proud to try it.

She kissed him back, accepting the fullness of his tongue. Her other hand crept to his shoulder and then glided over the thickly corded muscle there to his nape. She speared his thick hair with her fingers, cupping his skull, kissing him furiously, grateful for the practice she'd had in the past, all of which seemed to lead directly to this moment.

To this man.

He released her wrist and grasped her waist, pulling her into him again. And then they were moving. Moving as one. To his bed, she hoped. Maybe she could persuade him to give her a bit of relief. The ache that had been steadily building between her legs was more pronounced than ever, and his wicked lips moving over hers didn't help matters.

One step at a time, they went, as if it were a dance in a ballroom instead of a backward march across the Axminster. He was still kissing her when she heard something that sounded suspiciously like a door latch. But no, that couldn't be. Still kissing her until the moment he stopped and those strong hands of his lifted her gently into the hall.

He raised his head. "Go tae bed, lass."

His hands left her waist. She was bewildered. Bereft. The last thing she saw was his handsome countenance, his jaw tight as if he were using all the restraint he possessed.

And then the door closed in her face with a snap so abrupt that a small gust of wind buffeted her cheeks, making her stained skirts flutter around her legs.

She stared at the door, heart thudding in her breast.

And then she glared at it.

He had shoved her into the hall, the oaf. While kissing her, no less.

Madeline's eyes narrowed. Lachlan Macfie, Duke of Kenross, her future husband, had just declared war.

THE HOUSE PARTY was nearly at an end, and some of the guests had already departed, which meant that Lachlan found the garden blessedly empty the next morning when he eschewed breakfast in favor of taking the air and trying to talk some sense into his wee mind. He'd found his way to a large Venus fountain that was surrounded by miniature Cupids who ringed the edge, each of them emitting a perfect stream of water from their tiny doodles.

A damned peculiar fountain if you asked Lachlan. But apparently, it was centuries old, and the Duchess of Bradford had recently had it lovingly restored. He couldn't fathom why.

"Why is it that everyone at this house party seems to congregate around this bloody fountain?"

Lachlan glanced over his shoulder to find Decker approaching him on the path with that fluid ease and leonine grace that only true rakes—in Decker's case, a former true rake—possessed. It was a grace that a man of Lachlan's size would never own. He was forever slamming doors without realizing, lumbering about like a giant in a world of Lilliputians.

He sighed, but not because his friend had found him here, brooding. "Where else is a man tae congregate if not by a fountain presided over by tiny pissing Cupids?"

Decker chuckled, stopping when he'd reached Lachlan. "A question for the ages." He cocked his head. "But truly. What the devil are you doing out here this morning? Have you breakfasted?"

Lachlan's stomach rumbled. "I havenae just yet."

Denying his body's greatest pleasure—apparently aside from Madeline's hand on his cock—was his idea of penance. Because he wasn't proud of himself.

In fact, he was damned ashamed.

Just an hour closeted in his bedroom with Madeline Chartrand, and he'd already succumbed to base desire. But worse, he'd broken his vow to himself. This marriage was a carriage ride straight to hell.

He was doomed.

Aye, he may as well consign himself to the fires of Hades right now if he believed he would be able to withstand his future wife's seductive wiles.

Not. A. Chance.

"That isn't like you at all." Decker raised a brow, making an exaggerated show of peering into Lachlan's face. "Have you taken ill? Are you feeling feverish? Suffered another unfortunate blow to the head in castle ruins?"

"Another blow tae the head would be a mercy," he grumbled, passing a hand along his jaw and finding the prickle of stubble there.

He hadn't shaved this morning. He'd been too caught up

in his ruminations to have a care for aught else. It was a miracle he'd managed to dress himself, now that he thought on it.

Decker sobered, clearly understanding the gravity of the situation. "Why so Friday-faced this morning?"

"Because I did something stupid last night," he admitted, scrubbing at his jaw some more.

"Are you going to tell me, or must I guess?"

Lachlan grimaced. "I'd rather not say."

"Guesses it is, then." Decker's perennial good nature returned—the man couldn't resist a dark jest. "You walked naked through the great hall in your sleep?"

"Och, no."

"You broke wind near Lady Featherstone?"

Lachlan laughed reluctantly. "What do ye take me for? I'm a gentleman."

"Pity. I would have dearly loved to hear the lady's reaction if you had." Decker stroked his jaw in a pensive gesture. "Hmm, let me see. What else could you have done? You wrestled with a swan?"

"Nay. Not even a brute like me is man enough tae take on Honoré."

The disagreeable swan had been menacing the guests at Sherborne Manor for the entirety of the house party.

"You shaved your eyebrows?"

"Not again with my puir eyebrows." He pinned his friend with a glare. "Does it look like I shaved them tae ye?"

"I have no notion of how quickly those little beasties grow back," Decker said mildly. "For all I know, it happens within hours."

Lachlan chuckled despite himself. "Ye are a true arsehole, ye ken that, Elijah Decker?"

Decker bowed with an exaggerated flourish. "Happy to live up to my reputation, as always. Now, tell me what the devil has you so overwrought that you've forgone your mammoth breakfast and are frowning at a host of pissing Cupids."

Lachlan clenched his jaw, considering his words with great care. "I was indiscreet with Miss Chartrand."

"That's what has you so concerned?" Decker thumped him on the back. "Never fear, old friend. If you weren't sneaking about, pleasing your future wife, I'd be concerned."

"Och, well, I didnae please her," he grumbled, grim.

Heat prickled up the back of his neck and flooded his ears.

He couldn't bear to confess the rest. Not only did his honor as a gentleman preclude such a revelation, but he would drown in a sea of shame if he admitted to his friend that he'd been cad enough to allow his betrothed to take him in hand while offering her naught in return. Before promptly shoving her into the hall.

"So she didn't like what happened between the two of you?" Decker asked hesitantly. "Is that what's upset you?"

Good God, Madeline had loved it. Her enthusiasm had haunted his attempts at slumber. He'd never been with a woman who had been so artlessly free with her sensual nature before. It was nothing short of intoxicating. And that was also why it terrified him.

"There's something I've never told ye," Lachlan confided at last.

"I hope it doesn't involve leeches," Decker said wryly.

Lachlan winced. "Nay, it doesnae. But do ye recall when I told ye about Rose, the lass I left behind?"

Decker raised a brow. "I do. But what does that have to do with Miss Chartrand and your guilty face?"

"I loved Rose," he gusted out. "I wanted tae marry her. But she wanted tae marry someone wealthier. She wanted tae remain where she was instead of following me into the world tae see what I could make of myself. So, she stayed where she was, and she married the eldest son of an earl. It was a far better future than I could dream of giving her at the time. I was devastated when I left Scotland, ye ken. I vowed tae myself that I'd never again let a woman close. That I'd stay chaste as a monk for the rest of my days. And I have."

Lachlan finished his revelation in a rush.

Decker stared at him in silence.

And stared some more.

"Are ye no' going tae say anything?" Lachlan burst out when the quiet stretched between them.

"You're jesting," Decker said.

"I'm no' jesting," he said.

"*All* these years?"

Lachlan nodded grimly. "All these years."

"Bloody hell," his friend said, shaking his head. "You must have the fortitude of steel, old chum."

Not exactly.

Or perhaps he *had* possessed it. Until a fiery American had entered his life. Now, he was weaker than the silk he'd desecrated last night.

"I'm no' so certain I'll have the fortitude tae continue as I have," he continued. "Miss Chartrand is…"

His words trailed off as he struggled to define her.

Tempting.

Beautiful.

Sensual.

Lovely.

Unlike anyone he'd ever previously known.

"Your face says it all, my friend," Decker said, chuckling.

"And what does my face say, pray tell?" Lachlan demanded.

"That you're doomed." Decker was grinning now.

"Ye're enjoying this, ye bastard."

His friend laughed. "I'll admit, as a happily married man, I was wondering when you'd ever find yourself settled. I know you didn't want the dukedom or a wife, but this could be what you've been needing without ever realizing it."

"Of course it isnae," he groused. "I was perfectly content with my life just as it was. Working for ye has given me all the fulfillment I need."

"One would argue otherwise, given your reaction to Miss Chartrand," Decker countered. "Perhaps it's time to forget your vow."

"Never." His reaction was as instant as it was vehement. He would never forget how decimated Rose's rejection had left him. Nor would he ever present another woman with a chance to do the same. "Ye dinnae know what it was like, what I endured with Rose."

Decker's grin was wry. "You forget I've a past of my own, and if I hadn't allowed myself to fall in love with my wife, I would have missed the opportunity to spend the rest of my life with her. You need to marry Miss Chartrand. You may as well enjoy your marriage."

Lachlan sighed. "We'll have tae agree tae disagree on this matter, I'm afraid. I'm no' as resilient as ye."

"So you fear you'll fall in love with her, is that it?" Decker asked, far too perceptive as always.

"Och, no," he denied.

But the truth of it was, he did fear being vulnerable. Coming to care for her. He feared the damage a woman like Madeline could inflict upon his already bruised and battered heart. Or what remained of it.

"Some vows were meant to be broken, my friend," Decker advised him. "I think you'll find that this is such a one."

"Enough," Lachlan said. "Or I'll dump ye heid over arse into the drink, and then all the wee Cupids will be pissing on ye."

Decker laughed. "We can't have that. I'll say no more. The choice is yours. Will you look to the future, or will you allow the past to control you?"

What a damned question.

Lachlan didn't know the answer. He wasn't certain if he ever would. All he *did* know was that it would be a miracle if he lasted the next three weeks without ravishing Madeline Chartrand. Particularly if she stole into his room again.

The sensible, logical part of him hoped she wouldn't.

But another part of him—the part she'd so pleased the night before—decidedly hoped she would.

CHAPTER 7

That evening, Madeline made certain to wear her most becoming gown at dinner. It was a daringly cut scarlet evening gown that, coupled with the impressive tightlacing of her lady's maid, served to put her breasts on ample display. She wore ostentatious diamonds in her hair and at her ears and throat to help direct a certain male gaze should it prove elusive. And she also asked Vivi to be sure to seat her next to Lachlan.

Her loyal friend had granted Madeline her wish.

Which meant that, as the first course was laid before the remaining houseguests—an ever-diminishing assemblage—that evening, Madeline was to the right of Lachlan's large, warm presence. She had to admit that he looked extra handsome in his evening finery. The cut of his black coat served to complement his broad shoulders and chest perfectly. His red hair had been neatly combed and parted in the middle.

When he chose to, he played the role of gentleman quite well. She might even venture to say he looked quite ducal. But his debonair air aside, Madeline hadn't forgotten the way he had shoved her unceremoniously into the hall the night before. Nor had she failed to notice the way he had avoided her at breakfast and for the remainder of the day, aside from convening with her and her mother to establish the details of the wedding.

He may have conceded to marry her in three weeks' time, but he'd worn a funereal air that had made her long to stomp on his foot. Or kiss him. She'd alternated between the two. Thankfully, the Duke and Duchess of Bradford had been generous enough to allow them to stay on following the house party so that they might have the banns read.

From Yorkshire, Madeline would be departing for Scotland with her new husband, while Lucy would be journeying with their mother to Paris to prepare for her own lavish wedding to the Earl of Rexingham. The knowledge left Madeline feeling unsettled. She didn't want to carry on to Paris and find herself entangled in Mother's wedding of the century web. But she was also loathe to wave goodbye to her sister and mother and all the friends she possessed to accompany her new husband to a tumbledown castle in Scotland.

A new husband who wanted a marriage in name only and had announced his intention to uphold some ninny vow of celibacy.

And that meant she was either going to have to force Lachlan to cease being so stubborn and surrender to his attraction to her, or she was going to have to run away. As the latter option didn't particularly appeal to her—to say nothing of her father's fury should she do something so reckless—Madeline was left with little choice other than to seduce her future husband before they married.

Since he was currently ignoring her in favor of conversing with everyone at the table who wasn't Madeline, she was going to have to work harder at her efforts.

"Today was a lovely day, wasn't it, Your Grace?" she asked him directly, using her sweetest tone.

The one she reserved for when she truly wished to charm someone, or when she wanted to cozen someone into doing what she wanted. Madeline was employing all the weapons in her arsenal in this war.

He turned to her, searing her with his bright-blue stare. "Lovely, indeed."

And then he turned back to his soup.

This wouldn't do. A bowl of parsnip soup was most assuredly not more interesting than she was.

"What occupied you this morning?" she prodded. "I didn't see you at the breakfast table."

She had seen him most mornings during the house party. His appetite for breakfast was every bit as large as his appetite for salad. Perhaps larger. He'd become a legend over the last fortnight for his consumption of bacon and eggs. And yet, despite the informal breakfast hours that allowed guests to dine at their leisure, Madeline had been watching for him. He hadn't broken his fast as far as she had been able to tell.

"I went for a walk," he said mildly.

And then he stuffed a spoonful of soup into his mouth.

She narrowed her eyes at him. "A walk? Where did you go?"

He raised his brows at her, as if to say he couldn't speak because of the spoon. Never mind that he wasn't consuming the rich broth politely. Soup was meant to be delicately sipped from the spoon. Naturally, a man like Lachlan wouldn't concern himself with such trivialities.

But he was going to have to remove the silverware at some point.

Madeline folded her hands in her lap and waited, watching him serenely.

The spoon exited his sensual lips. "In the gardens."

"He was with me, I'm afraid," Mr. Elijah Decker intoned

from Lachlan's opposite side. "I was advising him on his future nuptials."

Madeline cast a searching glance in the direction of the dashing businessman. "I do hope your advice was sound, Mr. Decker."

"Never fear, Miss Chartrand," he said gallantly. "My counsel is always sound."

She wasn't sure she believed him. Mr. Decker had a certain whispered reputation. Apparently, he'd been something of a wild rake before settling down and falling in love with his wife, Lady Josephine. He looked like the sort of man who enjoyed getting into trouble.

"I wouldnae say it's always sound," Lachlan argued. "Mayhap half of the time."

"All the time," Decker countered smoothly.

"One-quarter of the time," Lachlan said.

Madeline watched the easy banter between the two friends and business associates. Their respect for each other was apparent, as was their affection. She found herself oddly envious of Mr. Decker's easy camaraderie with Lachlan. Her future husband seemed insistent upon keeping her at a distance, and she didn't like it.

"Always," Decker said, turning an adoring glance to his wife. "Isn't that right, *bijou?*"

Lady Josephine—Jo, as she was simply known in their circle—smiled at her husband, love shining in her eyes. "Of course it is. Without following your advice, I never would have found myself here at this table."

Lachlan grumbled something under his breath.

"What was that, dear friend?" Decker prodded, grinning. "I'm afraid I didn't hear you."

"Likely yer auld ears are no' functioning properly," Lachlan returned.

"Ha!" Decker laughed, the sound drawing the attention of

some of the other guests at the expansive dinner table who had been otherwise occupied in their separate conversations. "If my ears are indeed in poor condition, it's only down to all the doors you've been slamming all these years."

A curious redness was creeping along Lachlan's pronounced cheekbones. "Sometimes I dinnae know my own strength."

His embarrassment did something strange to Madeline. Left a faint trace of warmth in her chest. He was a complicated man. But beneath his brawny and brutish exterior, he had a tenderness that he hid from the world. She'd been privileged to witness it, the lowering of his guard, last night.

And she wanted to see it again.

"I'm grateful for your strength," she told him. "It saved my life in the castle."

"Och," he said, turning back to bestow the full force of his attention upon her again. "Ye're verra kind tae me, lass."

"I like being kind," she said quietly and with hidden meaning that was for him alone. "Especially to you, Your Grace."

The hue on his cheeks increased, and he looked away, but not before she spied the heat burning in the depths of his blue eyes.

Madeline turned her attention to her own bowl of soup, suppressing a smile.

He wasn't as unaffected as he pretended, then.

The rest of the dinner progressed splendidly, with Madeline roping Lachlan into conversation like a cowboy lassoing a calf.

By the time she retired for the evening, she felt certain she had outmaneuvered him. She'd caught him looking at her lips and the bold cut of her décolletage many times. She'd also been gratified that she had wrested his attention away from his friend and business associate with relative ease.

Madeline accompanied Lucy and their mother to Lucy's chamber and pleaded a headache when Mother wanted to spend some time discussing wedding details with her sister.

But instead of going to her chamber as she'd claimed, Madeline stealthily made her way to Lachlan's room. He'd stayed behind with some of the gentlemen to play billiards, which meant his chamber would be empty. She would be awaiting him when he retired for the evening again.

And it would be impossible for him to shove her into the hallway.

Because this time, she'd be waiting for him in his bed.

Naked.

Smiling to herself, Madeline slipped into his darkened room.

THE HOUR WAS LATE.

Lachlan was once again pleasantly soused.

He crossed the threshold of his guest chamber, half expecting to find Madeline awaiting him within, looking as glorious as she had at dinner in that brilliant red gown. He'd had to pick his jaw off the floor when he'd first seen her wearing it as they'd paired off to go into dinner. Her breasts were nothing short of perfection. He'd itched to weigh them in his palms. To see if her nipples matched the berry-stained color of her lips. To carry her away from the rest of the houseguests and make love to her all night long.

In the end, he hadn't done any of those things.

Nay, he had seized his restraint with both hands. He'd conversed with her like a gentleman, only allowing his gaze to slip to those luscious bubbies a handful of times. He'd kept his rampant erection under control. He'd been calm, measured, and cool.

And apparently, she had taken note of his efforts to maintain civility and to uphold his vow. Because she wasn't here in his chamber awaiting him, tucked into a wingback chair as he'd secretly hoped she might be.

He closed the door at his back, the low light from a lone lamp illuminating the empty chair in almost accusatory fashion. Lachlan tamped down the disappointment rising within, telling himself it was just as well that Madeline had not come to him again tonight. There was no knowing what he would have done had she been awaiting him.

He tugged at his necktie, feeling as if the stupid scrap of fabric was choking him. Best not to think about the folly that would have unfolded. He yanked the tie from his neck, tossing it atop a nearby table. And then he toed off his shoes before shucking his coat. He hadn't had the heart to play billiards this evening, so he had watched as Viscount Wilton had trampled the Marquess of Dorset, and likewise, Decker had trounced the Earl of Sinclair.

Diversions weren't what he needed. He'd been tippling some brandy to keep himself distracted. But that wasn't what he'd needed either. His cock was still annoyingly hard at the merest thought of Madeline, he still wanted her desperately, and even if she wasn't here in his chamber, he was still wedding her in less than three weeks' time.

With a sigh, he began undoing the buttons of his waistcoat. Unlike well-bred gentlemen—and most certainly unlike dukes—Lachlan didn't have a valet. He'd never concerned himself much with his dress. Even shaving was a task he performed on his own like an automaton with passable efficiency and no real discernment. He reckoned some things would never change, even if he had suddenly inherited a title and responsibilities he'd never wanted.

Also, a wife.

Lachlan removed his waistcoat and freed the buttons of

his shirt, trying to keep his mind from Madeline. By the rood, she'd been beautiful this evening, diamonds twinkling from her hair and her elegant throat. That gown. He'd wanted to tear it off her.

As if on cue, his rampant prick rose to attention.

There was no help for it; he was going to have to take himself in hand.

Grimly, he shrugged out of his shirt and turned, bare-chested, toward his bed.

And froze.

Because there, nestled beneath the coverlets on his bed, hair unbound in a gleaming chestnut cloud on his pillow, was Madeline Chartrand, soundly sleeping and—if her bare arm tucked over the counterpane was any indication—without a stitch of clothing.

Naked.

His cock's reaction was instant. He went harder than a ramrod, straining against his trousers, his breath quickening and his heart pounding into a rapid gallop in his chest. His body rejoiced at the rightness of seeing her in his bed, waiting for him, even if his mind knew he must not partake in the temptation awaiting him.

He watched her for a moment, her back to him, all that hair unraveled from the chignon she'd kept it in earlier. It was so long, lush, wavy tresses begging for him to sink his hands into, to wrap around his fist and hold her tightly as he ravished her mouth with fiery kisses. She was beautiful. And his. He moved toward her, drawn like a worthless hunk of metal to a magnet, even though he knew he shouldn't. That he ought to be keeping his distance, waking her discreetly, and demanding that she dress and leave his chamber for both their sakes.

It was the brandy that was ruling him now. Lulling him into a foolish haze of sensual promise. He couldn't think properly. His feet carried him around the bed to her side. Her face was lovely in the shadows, relaxed in sleep, her brow smooth as if she hadn't a care in the world. But then, likely, she didn't. She'd been born to one of the wealthiest men in America. Her biggest obstacle in life thus far had been her parents decreeing that she had to marry.

Their worlds couldn't have been more disparate. He couldn't bear to entrust himself to another woman, let alone one so ruled by capricious whims. She'd likely been horridly spoilt all her life, given whatever she wished. He had been born in genteel poverty, bearing the massive frame of his blacksmith ancestor, far removed from a title he'd never had a prayer of assuming.

And yet...

And yet, he couldn't resist reaching out to her. Gently trailing the backs of his fingers over her sinfully soft cheek.

"Madeline."

She stirred sleepily, her eyes remaining closed.

"Lass," he said more firmly, caressing her cheek again, finding a tendril of hair that had fallen over her face and sweeping it back. "Wake up."

"Mmm," she murmured, the hum doing wicked things to him.

It was throaty and husky, and it instantly made him wonder if she would make that same sound when she came.

Blast and damnation, this was not what he was meant to be thinking.

"Ye cannae be here again," he said more firmly, forcing sternness into his voice. "Ye cannae be in my bed."

Her eyes fluttered open at last, and she graced him with a sleepy smile that made his heart trip over itself. "I fell asleep."

"I ken." He tugged the covers that had slipped lower on her shoulder back up to her ear. "But ye need tae sleep in yer own room. In yer own bed."

She stretched her arms languidly over her head, a yawn slipping from her parted lips. "Why?"

"Why?" he repeated, incredulous. "This is it, lass. This is the moment my heid is going tae explode. Ye may wish tae hide, lest ye get all the splattery bits in yer lovely hair."

The cursed blankets were riding low again, the curve of one breast and the forbidden vee between them visible. Naturally, the vixen did nothing to rectify the matter. She simply left them there, a shocking amount of her glorious skin bared to his view.

"That sounds terribly messy," she said calmly. "Why don't you kiss me instead? I'd hate for your brains to go dashing all over the chamber. And I most especially wouldn't want them getting into my hair."

Lachlan stared at her. "Ye're a madwoman."

"I consider myself reasonably sane." She shifted in the bed, propping herself on her elbows and sending the counterpane perilously lower.

"Ye've been sent by the devil tae torment me," he grumbled, part of him praying that the bedclothes would continue their southward retreat and the other part of him praying they would remain in place. "Surely that's the answer. I must do penance for all my sins by continuously warding off the seductive wiles of a beautiful siren sent tae lure me intae the rocks like an unsuspecting sailor on a storm-tossed sea."

She smiled. "You think I'm beautiful?"

Bollocks. *That* was all she'd managed to extract from everything he'd just said?

"Are ye daft, woman? Of course ye're beautiful, and ye ken it well. Ye're also a she-devil come tae haunt my every waking hour."

And the sleeping hours too, but she didn't need to know that.

Her smile widened. She leveraged herself a bit higher on

her elbows. And the bedclothes surrendered, falling to her waist.

Lachlan forgot to breathe.

"Thank you. That's the nicest compliment I've ever been paid," she said. "Aside from the part where you called me a she-devil."

Her breasts were creamy and full. Not overly large and not too small. The perfect size for his hands. And her nipples *were* the same shade as her lips as he'd wondered, taut and tight and calling to his mouth.

He exhaled, then inhaled, feeling in the way he imagined a bull must when he was ready to rut. Beastly, his senses succumbing to fire. He wanted to charge. To claim.

"Lass," he hissed out, a desperate plea. "Ye should leave."

"But I'm quite comfortable here." Her smile turned wicked.

She knew what she was doing to him. The effect she had on him. And he was helpless to hide it. Helpless to stop the desire raging through him. To fight it.

"Move over," he gritted.

Madeline scooted to the right, positioning herself in the middle of the bed. He joined her against his better judgment. He was still wearing his trousers. That had to count for something. And he was atop the covers rather than beneath them.

"I was tired of looming over ye tae speak," he said, but that wasn't the whole truth and they both knew it. He was also desperate to be in this bed with her. "Now listen tae me lass, and listen clearly. Ye cannae be sneaking off tae my chamber like this, and ye most assuredly cannae be waiting for me in my bed wearing nary a stitch."

He had rolled to his side, facing her. She rolled onto her side as well, not bothering to cover her breasts. Her nipples pointed to him in erotic offering. He wanted to suck and lick them more than he wanted to live to see another day.

"I think I've proven that I *can* sneak into your chamber—and with ease," she said, a teasing note in her voice that somehow crept past his defenses.

He stared at her, realizing his power to resist her was disintegrating faster than those castle walls had back at the ruins. Decker's words that morning at the fountain returned to haunt him.

Will you look to the future, or will you allow the past to control you?

What if, all this time, he had been allowing Rose to control him from afar? He'd never thought of his vow that way before, but it was suddenly, abundantly clear. Rose had carried on with her life. She'd married—he knew that much. Likely, she'd had bairns of her own. And what had he done? He'd turned himself into a fortress, incapable of desire, of allowing anyone past his walls.

Maybe the time *had* come to look to the future.

"Lass," he said thickly. "If ye dinnae go now, I'll no' promise I'll be a gentleman."

"I don't want you to be a gentleman. And I don't want a marriage in name only."

Sweet heaven and hell and saints and angels and even the bloody rocks in the soil.

He was no match for this woman. He might be taller, larger, stronger. He might be a brawny brute who didn't know his own strength. But she had bested him. She had won.

He was giving in.

He reached for her, pulling her into him, his hand sliding under the blankets to find hot, sleek skin and wonderful curves. Her waist, the small of her back. Her breasts crushed into his bare chest, her nipples poking into him like hard little diamonds. He swept his hand up, along her spine, to cup her nape, capturing a handful of her sweetly scented hair. He pulled her head back, holding her there, looking deep into the depths of those gray eyes.

"Ye're sure?" he demanded gruffly.

"Kiss me and see," she invited.

And she didn't need to say it a second time. Lachlan's mouth claimed hers. The kiss was instantly ravenous, hungry, and hard. Her hands were on his body, coasting over his bare shoulders and down his back, as if she were starved for the feeling of him beneath her fingertips. He'd always felt ungainly, even before his vow of celibacy. But somehow, Madeline made him feel invincible, as if she reveled in his size, his strength.

It was intoxicating. Emboldening. With a groan, he fed her his tongue, and she sucked it greedily, opening for him, all velvet heat and lush welcome. He feasted on her mouth for what could have been seconds or hours. Kissed her until they were breathless and their bodies were writhing together on the bed in helpless need. Kissed her until he dragged his mouth along her jaw, down her throat, tugging her head back so that he could consume every inch of soft skin revealed to him.

Until finally, he reached her breasts. He sucked a nipple into his mouth, and she moaned, arching into him, her hips bucking into his. The friction against his rigid cock was divine torture. He wanted to be inside her so badly.

But that had to wait. He would pleasure her. He would do for her what he should have done when she'd come to his chamber before. The hand at her nape glided, traveling over the smoothness of her back, the supple curve of her delectable rump, over her hip. And then he rolled her to her back, still sucking her nipple as he went, his hand slipping between her legs.

She was wet.

Wet and hot.

And he had to taste her.

Lachlan kissed down her belly as she writhed under him. Every warning he'd issued to himself had been decimated by need. He was no longer capable of coherent thought. His lips devoured her.

"What are you…"

Her question trailed away when he impatiently shoved the counterpane away and shifted so that he could insert himself in the lee of her spread legs. His wide shoulders wedged between her thighs. The fit wasn't quite right, so he guided her legs over his shoulders and cupped her bottom in both hands, one arse cheek per palm.

"Oh," she said softly. "You're going to kiss me on my—"

"Damn it, lass," he ground out. "No' a word more."

Because if she said cunny, he'd spend in his trousers. And he wanted to savor the moment, to savor his Madeline, the woman who had somehow managed to tear him apart in less than a fortnight.

For once, she obeyed.

He pressed his face to the heart of her, inhaling her sweet, musky scent where she was pink and softer than any blossom he'd ever seen and where her desire was soaking her folds. And then he kissed her softly, slowly, making love to her with his mouth as she loosened under him, gasping in pleasure, her fingers finding their way into his hair, cupping his head as if to hold him there.

She needn't worry he would leave. She was better than anything he'd ever tasted. Like ambrosia from the gods, and he'd been far too long without the wondrous pleasure of making a woman come on his tongue. He would rectify that omission now, with this beautiful, bold hellion he intended to marry.

In his exuberance, he was certain he was lacking the proficiency he had once possessed for the task. But her body's reaction spurred him on, past any feelings of self-doubt. Lachlan remembered to listen to her sounds, to take his cues from the way her body undulated and stiffened and arched beneath his ministrations. When he licked her seam, she moaned softly. When his tongue found the plump bud of her clitoris, she inhaled sharply. And when he sucked as he had her nipple, she pumped into him, seeking more, his name falling from her lips.

"Oh, Lachlan."

Aye, he wanted to crow. *Say my name when you come.*

He might have, had his mouth not been presently, wonderfully filled with cunny. Slick, perfect, responsive, hot, delicate, demanding cunny. What a tragedy it would have been to die without experiencing this again, without experiencing *her*. Without having Madeline on his tongue, on his face. What had he been thinking when he'd naïvely supposed he could marry her without bedding her?

He couldn't even be in the same room with her and resist her.

He lost himself in pleasuring her, giving her everything she wanted. His tongue, his lips, his teeth, gently nibbling on her. When she came undone, it was with a choked cry, her thighs closing on his head, her body tensing and quivering under him, her fingers tightening in his hair. A gush of wetness flooded his mouth, ran down his chin. He lapped up her juices, devouring her in every way he could, returning to her pearl to suck and nip as she undulated against him, growing frenzied as the final waves of her release washed over her.

He sucked hard, wanting to torment her. Wanting her as desperate and mindless as she'd made him. And this time as he worked her perfect nub, he glanced up her body, finding her flushed and lovely, a sensual goddess in repose. Watching him.

Fuck.

His cock threatened to spill. He canted his hips and pressed his throbbing erection into the mattress, staving off his own release. Because he wanted to give her another. And this time, he wanted her eyes on him. He wanted her to watch what she'd made him do. What she'd reduced him to.

And if he could hold off his spend for long enough, he'd make her come a third time too.

CHAPTER 8

*S*he had unleashed a beast.

A feral, wonderful Scottish beast whose handsome face was currently buried between her thighs. He sucked on the throbbing bud of her sex, eliciting another delicious rush of pleasure over her. And this time, he held her gaze, his blue eyes keeping her in his thrall, his stare burning and hot and dark with lust.

She couldn't look away.

It was as if he commanded her to watch. And that unspoken mastery somehow heightened her pleasure to an unbearable level. Until she was soaring again, a new bliss cresting over her, thrashing and wild under his mouth.

"Lachlan," she choked out. "Lachlan."

"Aye, lass," he growled against her soaked center. "Come again for me."

"A-again?" She was breathless, so overwhelmed by her body's reaction that her very ears were ringing.

It seemed a sheer impossibility for her to achieve more pleasure than he'd already visited upon her. But Lachlan had other ideas. He was still there, his wicked mouth pleasuring her, lapping, sucking, pressing. Licking, giving, biting. One of his big hands left her bottom, and then she felt a new pressure at her entrance as his finger sank inside her.

All the while, he kept up his relentless pleasuring, devouring her as if she were the finest feast ever to have been laid before him. Oh, the sinful man. The sinful, delicious man. That feeling was somehow coiling within her. She was ready to explode.

Another thrust of his finger deep inside her, making her huff a gasp and a moan all at once. He sucked on the exquisitely sensitive bundle of flesh hidden in her folds. Sucked hard and sucked long, and that lone finger sank deeper still until she cried out his name, thrashing and twisting as sheer bliss hit her and everything tightened and spasmed, her vision flecked with tiny glittering stars that convinced her for a delirious moment that, together, they somehow had set off fireworks on the Sherborne Manor lawn and they were now exploding into the night sky.

But that was fanciful and silly.

There were no fireworks. There was only herself and the brawny Scot who had just thoroughly pleasured her and upended her world. Her heart was pounding, her head was roaring, her body was throbbing, and her breaths were ragged, torn from her.

"Lachlan," she murmured his name again, thinking it would be almost impossible for her to form any other words, any thoughts that weren't him and what he'd just done to her.

She would agree to marry him again just for this.

"Ah, lass," he rasped, moving from between her legs at last, lying on his back at her side on the bed, still wearing nothing but his dark trousers from earlier that evening.

The muscles in his broad chest rippled as he breathed in and out as heavily as she did. That was when she noticed the thick ridge pressing against the fall of his trousers. And all the naughty things she'd read about returned to her, along with the desire to please him as well. To make certain he no longer wanted a marriage in name only from her. To be sure there would be much more of this passion in their future.

She reached for him hesitantly, settling her hand over the straining placket of his trousers.

"Och," he grunted, his body stiffening under her touch. "Lass, what are ye doing?"

"I want to please you," she said.

"Ye please me already. Verra much."

She liked the way he said that word, verra. Liked the way his burr rolled off his tongue.

"I want to please you more," she insisted, reaching for the fastening on his trousers and plucking a button free of its mooring.

"Lass."

There was warning in his tone, but there was surrender too. And desire. She ignored the warning in favor of the rest, plucking more buttons undone until his trousers were open and she found the slit in his smalls, releasing his cock, which was hard and impossibly large and straining for her touch.

This time, she shifted, sidling down the bed so that she was nearer to him.

"Ye dinnae—" he began, only for her to silence his protest by pressing a kiss to the bulbous head of his impressive cock.

"Madeline," he repeated. "This isnae necessary."

"But it is." Smiling, she gripped him in her hand, stroking him as she knew he liked.

He made a strangled sound, his lips parting, his eyes glazing over with passion.

The same small bead of pearlescent moisture had seeped from the slit on the tip of him again, and this time, she gave in to her curiosity, flicking her tongue over it, lapping it up.

He mumbled something unintelligible, which she considered an excellent sign he was enjoying himself, so she grew bolder and took the tip of him into her mouth.

The stream of curses that escaped him was decidedly blasphemous.

Madeline continued her exploration of him, taking him deeper and sucking gently.

"Ah, lass."

The words were a growl torn from him. He was losing control, and she liked it. He seemed to be lengthening and thickening in her mouth and hand—another sign that what she was doing gave him pleasure. His hips pumped under her in shallow thrusts, and she tried to oblige him by taking more of him into her mouth, but he was far too large. She gagged, drawing back to catch her breath, embarrassed by her body's sudden reaction.

"I'm sorry," she apologized, hoping he wouldn't think she'd gagged because she hadn't been enjoying herself.

For pleasuring him was making the ache between her legs renew itself with determined vigor.

"Ye neednae apologize, lass," he said, voice ragged with desire. "It's a compliment."

That took her by surprise. "It is?"

"Aye." He grinned. "The size of a man's cock is a private vanity."

Her hand was still wrapped around the base of him, so she stroked appreciatively. "I had no notion, but it makes sense now, when I think upon all the ladies in the books exclaiming nonsensical things like *what a big tool you have.*"

A rusty-sounding chuckle stole from him. "Och, lass. Ye'll be the death of me. Come here."

He held his hand out to her. "But you haven't…"

"I neednae."

His cock—thick, heavy, pulsing in her hand—suggested otherwise.

"Shall I use my hand instead of my mouth?" she offered.

He closed his eyes, groaning low, looking as if he were in agony. "Dinnae say such things, or I'll lose what control I have remaining."

But that was the thing. She liked when this big, powerful Scot lost control. Madeline stroked him again as he'd shown her he liked, tightening her grip. But when she bent to take him in her mouth once more, he groaned again and shifted suddenly, his movements so quick that in a blink, she was flat on her back with him straddling her.

"Not in yer mouth. Not before we're at least married," he elaborated. "Lovely as it feels, I'd never forgive myself. There's another way, if ye wish tae try..."

Another way? Excellent news. She hadn't realized there were so many options for lovemaking. The books were quite descriptive, but after a time, their naughty scenes took on a similitude that bored her.

"Of course I wish to try," she reassured him. "Show me."

The positioning of their bodies was new as well. Although he straddled her, he bore his weight on his knees. She was pinned neatly beneath his hulking form, and yet there was no pressure. She could slip away at any moment she chose. But he was still wearing his trousers, which made her frown until he took his cock in hand and gave himself a firm stroke.

"Take yer hands and press yer breasts taegether," he told her, voice low and rumbly and decadent.

She did as he asked, cupping her breasts and crushing them together so that they looked much larger and fuller than they ordinarily were. That pleased Madeline, for she'd often bemoaned her own endowment. Bodices never fit her quite as snugly in that area as she would have preferred.

"Like this?" she asked, drinking in the sight of him, so potent and virile.

So wickedly handsome and fully roused, his length rigid and ruddy as his big hand stroked up and down, his jaw held so tightly that a muscle ticked there. Seeing him so undone was the most potent aphrodisiac. And to think, *she* was the cause of it—that only served to make her feel even more powerful, more desirable.

"Aye, like that," he gritted. "Keep them that way."

And then, he astonished her by gliding his cock between her breasts. The sensation was pleasant. Surprising. The thickness of him, the heat, the smooth length, the wetness of the seed leaking from him painting her skin. She rubbed her nipples with her thumbs as he thrust in and out of the plumpness of her breasts, his rhythm increasing, low sounds of pleasure spilling from his lips.

How intriguing. She'd never imagined such a thing possible. She liked it. As he worked himself in and out, she played with her nipples, overly sensitive now, keeping her breasts firmly pressed together. Lachlan didn't last long. His entire body stiffened as he thrust one more time, and then with a moan and another curse, he withdrew. Gripping himself firmly, he spent on her breasts, the hot lash of his seed filling her with a new ache. How she wanted more.

More and more and more.

It seemed she could never have enough with him.

As if she were insatiable.

He was breathing heavily as he rolled to his back at her side, crashing into the mattress with so much force that she bounced and the headboard smacked off the wall.

"By the rood," he grumbled, tucking himself back into his trousers and hastily buttoning his falls. "I'm sorry, lass."

"Don't be," she reassured him, fascinated by what had just happened between them.

Also not quite knowing what to do with the spend covering her naked skin.

As if he'd heard her unspoken question, Lachlan rose from the bed and strode across the room, returning to her with a cloth he'd dampened at the washbasin and gently, methodically cleaning his seed from her. She watched him from beneath lowered lashes as he performed the task, a flush stealing over his cheekbones.

"I shouldnae have done that," he added, self-loathing lacing his voice.

"I'm glad you did." She reached for his wrist, staying his cleansing. "Lachlan, look at me."

With a sigh, he forced his gaze to hers. "Aye?"

"That was wonderful. Much better than the books."

He shook his head, a rueful grin curving his lips upward. "Och. A fine hellion I've found myself. I've never met another woman quite like ye, Madeline Chartrand."

She smiled back at him, newly aware of her own nudity now that the raging fires of their mutual passion had dampened. "Thank you. I pride myself on being an original. Now, then." She reached for the abandoned counterpane and pulled it over herself for modesty's sake. "Do you think we might have a talk about this vow of yours?"

His jaw hardened again, and he slipped from the bed, crossing the room to dispense with the sullied cloth. When he returned, there was fire in his eyes and determination in the firm set of his sensual lips. He was also wearing his shirt, quite spoiling her unabashed enjoyment of his muscled chest.

"Please?" she pressed, shifting herself into a partially seated position, holding the counterpane as a shield.

He sat gingerly on the edge of the bed, as if he feared she were a serpent who intended to strike at any moment. "Och, lass."

He didn't want to speak about it. Fair enough. But she *did*, and if they were going to be married, she wanted to know as much about this man as possible, beyond the physical intimacy they'd shared.

"Why did you want a marriage in name only with me?" she persisted. "Do I not please you? Do you not find me attractive?"

She was reasonably sure she knew the answer to the latter questions already, but her pride wanted to hear the affirmation from him.

"Never that," he reassured her, looking as tense as he sounded. "Dinnae think for a moment that ye dinnae please me—ye please me verra well, as ye can see from how little control I have in yer presence. And as for yer looks, let me assure ye that ye're the bonniest lass I've ever known."

"Then why?" she asked, needing to know and yet suspecting she didn't truly want the answer.

He scrubbed at his jaw. "Because I loved a lass once."

That wasn't what she had wanted to hear. The notion of Lachlan loving another woman filled her with sudden, unexpected jealousy. She thought of his admission when he'd first proposed.

"Was it the other woman you asked to marry you?" she asked carefully, tamping down her emotions.

"Aye." He paused, his countenance turning wry. "But she chose another man over me. One who she was sure would give her the life she wished tae lead."

He'd been thrown over for someone else.

Her brow furrowed as she imagined the pain he must have been dealt by the inconstancy of the woman he'd loved. Likely not so different from the pain she'd endured when she had realized Charles had been cozening her. Using her to gain her fortune and her father's power and prestige. A liar.

"She married another man instead of you?" she asked, trying to understand.

Needing to, so that she could navigate this looming marriage of theirs.

"Aye, she did. One who was wealthier, more powerful, and far more handsome than I ever could have hoped tae be."

She didn't believe the woman he loved could have found anyone more compelling than Lachlan. But that was another matter.

"What did you do then?" she asked.

"I left Scotland. Left behind the life I knew. I came here, tae England. I found Decker, and before long, I'd found my way at last in this mad world of ours. At least, I thought I had. Until word reached me about Kenross."

He was still frowning, his blue eyes clouded by the pain of his past, as if he had returned to that time and place within his mind.

She reached for him, laying a hand on his arm. "This woman you loved. Is she still in Scotland?"

He inhaled sharply, as if the action caused him pain. "Aye, lassie. She is. But ye neednae fret. That door closed long ago."

She wasn't so certain. If the door had indeed closed, then why had he failed to move on with anyone else? Why had he made the vow to himself, and why had he wanted a marriage in name only with her? Madeline had so many questions, so few answers. But there was one question rising inside her, far more important than all the rest.

One she needed answered.

Tonight.

"Do you still want a marriage in name only with me?" she asked him quietly, holding her breath as she awaited his response.

Slowly, he shook his head, the sadness leaving his eyes in favor of something she couldn't define. "Nay, lass. Ye've proven tae me that I havenae the fortitude I mistakenly believed I possessed where ye're concerned."

His tone was wry.

Madeline smiled. "I'm glad."

"Aye, I am as well, lass." His voice was gruff yet tender. "But for all that, ye need tae dress yerself and get yer arse out of my room. And do no' come back until we're good and truly wedded."

His stern admonishment made her smile widen. "You can't resist me. Admit it."

"Ye've seen the evidence yerself." He surprised her by leaning over her on the bed and giving her a swift kiss. "Come, lass. I'll help ye tae dress."

He took her hand in his, lacing his fingers through hers.

Madeline stared down at their entwined hands, hoping this was the beginning of something bigger and better than either of them had imagined.

"Look at my lad, fully grown into a man, soon to be married. The day is coming ever closer, you know."

Decker's teasing voice set Lachlan's jaw on edge as he glared at him across the billiards room. "Watch yer tongue. I'd hate tae cut it out."

"What?" Decker feigned scandalized horror. "Is it wrong of me to feel like a proud papa watching his son going off to find his way in the world?"

"Like a proud papa, my arse," Lachlan grumbled. "We're of an age, ye ken."

"Och, I reckon we are," Decker mocked with a terrible attempt at mimicking Lachlan's Scottish accent.

"Ye sound nothing like me," he said proudly as he scored.

"True. I speak English, for one thing." Decker took aim, grinning, scoring a point with ease. "But all jests aside, old friend. I'm happy to see you and Miss Chartrand getting along well these days. It gives me hope for your future together."

The future was decidedly different than Lachlan had imagined it would be, even months ago. He had been content in his life. Happy to bury himself in work. To verbally parry Decker's insults about his eyebrows and slam doors and help oversee his friend's many business ventures.

Returning to Scotland had been the last thing on his mind, and as for taking a wife? He'd been convinced he would never do it. To say nothing of becoming intimate with a woman again. He had persuaded himself that part of his life had been unnecessary, not worth the potential harm it caused, and casual indiscretions had never been one of his peccadilloes.

But Madeline had shown him differently.

And that terrified him. Secretly, of course. It also exhilarated him.

"Miss Chartrand is a good woman," he said now as he angled his cue, trying not to think of all the naughty visits she'd been paying to his chamber, lest he miss his mark. "I cannae say I deserve her, but I'll be happy tae make her mine just the same."

The days had settled into a routine for Lachlan. Not precisely a comfortable one. But a necessary one, now that he had reconciled himself to the fact that he would be having not just a wife in name only, but a wife in every sense of the word.

The houseguests dispersed, the party at an end, leaving just himself, Decker and Lady Jo, the Earl and Countess of Sinclair, the Duke and Duchess of Bradford, and Madeline, her mother, and her sister in residence.

Somehow, he and Madeline had managed to evade notice. The more Lachlan pleaded with her to observe propriety until they were married, the more determined the minx was to circumvent him. Only yesterday, she had cornered him in the garden maze, and he'd been so overwhelmed with desire that he had gone to his knees before her and buried his head under her skirts. It had been one of the most wicked and glorious moments of his life, and it had been worth the gravel imprints he'd sported on his poor knees afterward.

"Marriage is a blissful state," Decker said, taking aim with his cue stick after Lachlan failed to score a point. "Take it from me, old chap. Without my wife, I would be nothing. If you find even a modicum of the happiness I've discovered with Jo, you'll be the second happiest man alive."

Lachlan grunted, not as convinced. "And I'll assume ye're the happiest, then?"

Decker slanted a grin in his direction, striking the ball with fluid grace without even watching and scoring anyway. "Can you doubt it? You knew me before Jo."

"Och, aye, I did. And a right grumpy bastard ye were then."

His friend chuckled and pressed a hand to his heart in a dramatic gesture. "I'm wounded."

"It's true," Lachlan insisted.

For it was, and they both knew it. Lady Jo was an angel among women who had swept into his jaded friend's life, made him fall in love with her, and banished all the bitterness and pain of his past. Decker and Lady Jo were a different matter, however. Lachlan wouldn't find himself in such a circumstance. He was impervious to love; it caused nothing but agony, and he wanted no part of it.

"Fine," Decker allowed grudgingly. "I was a grumpy bastard before her. But the same might be said for you."

Lachlan glowered at him. "I'm no' a grump."

"Not a grump, perhaps. But I know you. The happy, jesting face you show the world hides the darkness of your past."

Decker's words struck uncomfortably close to the truth.

Lachlan sighed heavily and eyed the balls on the baize, trying to map out his next shot and failing miserably. "Dinnae go trying tae write my life intae a fairy tale, Decker. I'm as content as I can be."

"But you're giving Miss Chartrand a chance, are you not?" Decker pressed.

"A chance tae what, destroy me?" Lachlan snorted. "Decidedly no' because I'm smarter than that."

"You've clearly broken your vow, however," his friend added shrewdly. "And I commend you for it. It was a bloody stupid thing to do, taking a vow of celibacy." He shuddered. "Christ, old friend. You're not a monk."

Madeline had proven to him that he wasn't.

Heat crept up the back of his neck. "A gentleman never tells tales."

"I didn't ask for tales. What do you think I am?" Decker gestured toward the billiards table with his chin. "Are you going to take your turn before I go to my eternal reward?"

He grumbled at his friend's good-natured admonishment. "Yer hyperbole is ridiculous."

Lachlan took his aim finally, managing to score a point.

"*I'm* ridiculous," Decker said unapologetically. "It's one of my best traits."

"According tae ye and who else?" he countered.

"My darling wife, of course," Decker answered smoothly. "Ask her, and I'm sure she'd be ready to sing my praises."

Lachlan laughed. "I'm going tae miss yer daft notions."

Decker straightened, his countenance going serious. "I'm going to miss you too, old friend. Hell, I don't know what I'll do without you now that you're returning to Scotland. And as a duke, no less."

Returning to Scotland. As a duke. It was a sobering real-ization, one he'd been doing his damnedest not to think about as he'd become caught up in the whirlwind of his betrothal and getting better acquainted with Madeline. It would be strange, indeed, returning to his home after so long.

"Ye're welcome tae come and pay us a visit any time," he said, striking thoughts of what his return to Scotland would truly mean from his mind. "As soon as Madeline's fortune turns Kenross Castle back into a home rather than a moldy pile of rubble, that is."

"Say the word, and we'll be there," Decker assured him.

Lachlan nodded, feeling his throat go tight with suppressed emotion. "Thank ye. Now, let's get back to this billiard game so I can finish trouncing yer sorry arse."

His friend laughed, and the heaviness of the moment passed.

But the knowledge that he was about to leave the life he'd known for so long behind remained with Lachlan, like a boulder lodged behind his breastbone. He could only hope that his marriage with Madeline wouldn't be as doomed as his romance with Rose had been.

CHAPTER 9

hree interminable weeks of sneaking in and out of Lachlan's chamber had finally come to an end. Madeline took a sip of her wine and glanced around the table at the friends who had joined them for their impromptu wedding breakfast. Lord and Lady Sinclair were in attendance, as were Mr. Decker and Lady Jo. There was also, of course, Vivi and her husband, the duke, and a rather wan-looking Lucy, seated beside their proudly beaming mother.

Lachlan was a strong, comforting presence at Madeline's side.

At long last, they were husband and wife.

She was the Duchess of Kenross.

Lachlan's bride.

She hoped they hadn't both made a dreadful mistake. The morning had begun inauspiciously enough, but thereafter, everything had descended into chaos. Terrible rain had begun to fall, leaving her gown's train muddied and water-logged after she passed through the courtyard between Sherborne Manor and its small chapel. The lake was overflowing its banks. Cracking thunder had overshadowed their vows as if even the heavens objected to their marriage.

Lachlan had gently teased her about being bad luck for her gowns. Her cheeks had gone hot as she'd recalled in vivid detail precisely how he had ruined one of said gowns. Mother had spied it and wondered if she was bilious. Honoré the swan had somehow made his way into the manor house, and he'd led the butler on a merry chase in the great hall, hissing and carrying on and even leaving a squishy pile of excrement behind that no one had taken note of until Madeline had stepped in it.

Her father had been too concerned with his work to journey from New York City for the nuptials, and since Lucy's wedding to the earl would be much less rushed, he was choosing to attend hers instead. Not even her brother Duncan had come, too caught up in being Father's apprentice, no doubt, to venture from his side as he prepared to take over their father's empire.

As if sensing her disquiet, Lachlan covered her hand with his and leaned near so that he could murmur in her ear without anyone overhearing. "Ye make a lovely bride, Madeline."

Gratitude swept over her. In truth, she was sodden, her silk gown was likely ruined from the rain and mud, and her hair was dreadfully frizzed after being caught in the rain and then drying. But he made her *feel* lovely.

"Thank you." She cast an appreciative gaze over his brawny form. "You make a braw groom."

"Look at ye, already learning yer Scottish," he teased lightly.

They'd grown quite close over the past few weeks. And not just in the physical sense—although there had been a great deal of that as well. Everything but the consummation of their marriage, which he had steadfastly insisted must be after they were wed. No amount of persuasion or attempted seductions on her part had swayed him. Lachlan had become quite adept at distracting her from her intended course by wicked means.

Not that she was complaining.

But they had also become almost friends. Given the rushed nature of their betrothal and wedding, it was far more than she had expected. And the more time she spent in Lachlan's presence, the more she grew to like him. The more she grew to like him, the more concerned she was that she was falling under her new husband's spell. While he, despite his disarming charm and infallible ability to bring her pleasure, remained emotionally distant.

"I may as well learn it," she told him now, forcing a smile for his benefit. "I'll be there soon enough."

"Aye, ye will." A shadow passed over his countenance, his jaw hardening.

She wondered what he was thinking about and hoped it wasn't the woman who had broken his heart. Scotland was a vast place. Surely they wouldn't cross paths with her upon their return. Madeline banished the notion, dismissing it as her nervousness over the impending changes looming before her.

Not only was she a wife, but she was leaving England for Scotland.

For a derelict castle she had never seen.

She knew precious little about what awaited her. Even Lachlan seemed torn between excitement at their journey to his homeland and dispassionate calm.

"You're certain you'll make the journey back to London for my wedding to Rexingham, won't you?" Lucy asked from across the table, poking at the elegant assortment of food on her plate but not eating it.

"Of course I will," Madeline reassured her. "I wouldn't miss your wedding, dearest."

Lucy nodded, offering her a tight smile, and Madeline felt a pang in her heart for her sister's future. The Earl of Rexingham, for all that he was a cold and proper man, had drawn Lucy to him somehow. They'd certainly engaged in enough passionate embraces to make it imperative that they wed. Madeline hoped that Lucy would find contentment with her husband.

Just as she hoped she would find some measure of peace in her own future with her new husband.

How strangely their worlds had changed since they had arrived at Sherborne Manor weeks ago. Madeline certainly hadn't expected to find herself here, at the side of a brawny Scot, as his wife. But here she was, and she honestly could say that she didn't regret a single moment of it.

"No wandering about in castle ruins in Scotland, if you please," Lucy said sternly, before casting a protective, sisterly stare in Lachlan's direction. "I trust you'll keep my sister safe and out of trouble, won't you?"

Lachlan gave Madeline's hand a squeeze, smiling at Lucy. "Ye have my word I'll always keep yer sister safe. Now, as for keeping her out of trouble... Ye *do* know yer sister, dinnae ye?"

His cheeky question earned a smile from Lucy. "That's an excellent point. Madeline does like to get into scrapes."

"Coming from you, that's rich." Madeline couldn't help but tease her sister in return.

After all, it was Lucy's midnight assignation with a footman gone awry that had led to her impending marriage to the Earl of Rexingham. To say nothing of the other scandals she'd intentionally caused on both sides of the Atlantic. Yes, Madeline supposed that the Chartrand sisters made quite a pair. Little wonder Mother was pleased to be marrying them off.

"I'll thank you not to speak of it," Lucy said archly.

"Girls, that is quite enough of your squabbling," Mother chastised, intervening as she often did whenever Madeline and Lucy argued. "I'm pleased to see my daughters so well settled, Madeline with your duke and Lucy with Lord Rexingham before long. It brings a tear of joy to my eye."

"Perhaps you have an eyelash in your eye," Lucy offered unkindly.

Emotion was indeed quite rare for Mrs. William Chartrand. Madeline wasn't sure she'd ever witnessed their mother in a moment of vulnerability. Her protective shell was harder than a turtle's.

Mother ignored Lucy, raising a handkerchief to her eye and dabbing as if she were overcome with sentimental joy. In fact, she was probably crying tears of happiness as she contemplated the various means through which she would be able to lord her daughters' astounding marital coups over the rest of society back home in New York.

But Madeline quite wisely refrained from saying so aloud.

"All I can say is thank you to the wonderful and generous Duke and Duchess of Bradford, for hosting us and allowing us to marry here at Sherborne Manor," Madeline offered instead, turning her gaze to their host and hostess, who made a very handsome and much-in-love pair.

Madeline was thrilled to see her friend so happy after a period of estrangement from her husband. No one deserved contentedness more than Vivi, and she wore it well. She positively vibrated with happiness.

"It was our pleasure," Bradford said easily, turning an adoring gaze on his wife. "And everyone knows that my darling Vivi can't resist the opportunity to host her friends for a worthy cause. In this case, it was both the Lady's Suffrage Society and, it would seem, love."

Love for Vivi and Bradford, unquestionably. But not for Madeline and Lachlan. She tamped down a fresh surge of envy. And it wasn't a love match for Lucy and her earl, or for Edith and Mr. Blakemoor either. Even if Clementine and Dorset, along with Wilton and Charity, had fallen madly in love. Perhaps acceptance of their fates was all the rest of the friends could hope for as they faced uncertain futures as wives. Madeline knew she was more fortunate than some.

At least Lachlan hadn't tricked her into marriage as Blakemoor had done to Edith. And at least she wasn't forced to endure Mother's wedding of the century nonsense as Lucy was. Besides, Madeline enjoyed Lachlan's company—likely more than she should, given that he was firmly guarding his past from her. And the pleasure he could bring her...

Well, she enjoyed that very much.

Her cheeks were heating at the thought, so she took a hasty sip of her wine to distract herself.

"I'm so happy to have brought together my dearest friends," Vivi was saying, her eyes gleaming with suppressed emotion as she spoke to the table. "And to celebrate the Lady's Suffrage Society. We are, all of us, stronger together."

"Hear, hear," Bradford said, raising his glass in salute.

Everyone around the table raised their glasses as well, and more toasts were made. Madeline spent the rest of the wedding breakfast drinking too much wine and hoping that the lashing rain and dreadful luck of the day wasn't an ominous sign of what was to come.

LACHLAN WAS EXHAUSTED as the train rattled over tracks taking them north in their sumptuous private car. The use of the car was a wedding gift from Decker and Lady Jo, and the privacy and comfort it provided on their journey was appreciated. The trip itself, however, was a source of some consternation.

His return to Scotland was bittersweet. Tucked against his side was Madeline, who had somehow fallen asleep, lulled, he supposed, by the endless motion of the train gliding on its tracks. Undoubtedly, the overwhelming nature of the morning, their wedding, and the breakfast that had followed had contributed. They'd been traveling for some time now, the scenery passing by in a torpid blur of green grass, brown mud, and gray skies, her head on his shoulder a welcome weight.

It was almost impossible to believe that the stunning, fiery, unpredictable woman at his side was his wife.

By the rood, not just his wife.

She was his duchess now. He needed to remember he was the Duke of Kenross, even if it didn't feel as if he was. Because, like it or not, his entire life as he'd known it—and loved it—was about to change irrevocably. Traveling to Edinburgh over the next few hours was only a part of their journey. From Edinburgh, they would be hiring a carriage and traveling to Castle Kenross.

Or what remained of it.

Lachlan grimaced as he thought of the uncertain fate awaiting the both of them. As if sensing his mood, Madeline shifted against him, and he could tell the instant she awakened.

"Good morning to ye," he drawled, opting for good humor.

The truth of it was, he was more than a wee bit terrified of being a husband. Of being alone with her. No barrier of honor to keep him from claiming what he wanted. All the guards he'd kept carefully in place about to fall.

Because he couldn't afford to care for her too much. He wouldn't put himself in such a vulnerable place again.

She straightened and stretched, giving him a soft smile that made him want to kiss her as she shifted away from him. "How long was I asleep?"

"An hour or so," he guessed. "We've no' too much farther to travel now, by the look of the land beyond the window."

They had made the customary stops on their journey, but even without consulting his pocket watch, Lachlan knew they were close to their destination for the evening.

"I'm sorry for sleeping on you like that," she apologized, a pretty tinge of pink gilding her cheekbones. "I do hope I didn't do anything embarrassing like snore or drool on your coat sleeve."

He laughed at her words rather than her worry. "I wouldnae have minded if ye had, lass, but ye neednae worry. My sleeve is far safer than yer puir gowns have been in my presence."

Madeline chuckled softly, the sound doing strange things to his insides. "My train was in a dreadful state today, wasn't it? Fortunately, I could detach it and leave it behind for my mother to contend with. But the rain and mud were hardly your fault."

Still, he couldn't help but to feel as if he were somehow to blame. He was responsible for Madeline now, in a way he hadn't been responsible for another soul since his dear mother had gone to her reward. For many years, it had been naught but the two of them, his father having died when Lachlan had been but a bairn. And then, it had been just Lachlan after his mother's short illness and decline. He'd been alone. Until he'd fallen in love with Rose.

Only, that love had left him more alone than ever. He'd traveled aimlessly, going wherever the wind blew after he'd left Scotland in search of himself until he'd found Decker.

Now, for the first time, he had a wife. A woman whose happiness depended upon him. A woman to protect, to kiss, to cherish.

To bed.

But he wouldn't think about that just now, lest his randy prick get any unseemly ideas. It wouldn't do to tup his wife for the first time in a damned train car.

He forced a smile for Madeline's benefit, hoping she wouldn't sense the worry weighing him down. "As yer husband, I'm responsible for ye now, gowns and all."

Husband. How strange that word felt on his tongue, speaking it in relation to himself. But it was true. They were married. Madeline was his wife. Nothing was standing between them, save his common sense now. If he possessed any at all.

Madeline was staring at him in a considering fashion, and he shifted on his seat, discreetly adjusting his trousers, which were growing snugger beneath her regard. "Responsible for me? You make me sound like a chore."

Och, he was making a muck of it.

"Never a chore," he reassured her, reaching out to brush a stray tendril of hair from her cheek. "A blessing."

Her skin was soft and silken, and he couldn't deny the jolt that went through him at the contact. He wanted to keep touching her, but he didn't dare, for fear he'd entirely lose control.

She raised a brow. "My dowry is a blessing, you mean."

"Yer dowry is but a benefit of marrying ye," he said gallantly. "I'll no' lie about needing it. Ye ken that's why I asked for yer hand from the start. But over the last few weeks, I've come tae admire ye greatly, lass. Marrying ye was my privilege. Being yer husband is an honor."

It startled Lachlan to realize how earnestly he meant those words. He wasn't merely saying it to spare her feelings.

He liked Madeline. She was a good sister, a faithful friend, and she was damned intelligent. To say nothing of her beauty, which was undeniable. She made him laugh. She made him want her. She made him feel alive again in ways he hadn't remembered were possible.

"That was quite sweet of you to say." Madeline smiled at him, and he wanted to kiss her badly. "But you needn't pay me any unnecessary flattery. I know quite well why you married me. Now, tell me about this castle of yours. Is it uninhabitable?"

Her swift change of subject had him blinking, forcing him to realize that his hand had lingered at her cheek. He withdrew it now and straightened, reminding himself that he had no intention of bedding his new wife on a train.

"I'm told Castle Kenross is in a bad way," he said, passing his hand along his jaw ruefully as he was forced to think about the sad state of affairs awaiting them.

"You're told," she repeated, her brow furrowing. "Do you mean to say that you haven't seen it for yourself yet?"

Her surprise was evident, and he knew a moment of guilt and shame at his own actions. In his defense, inheriting a dukedom and all that it entailed hadn't been what he'd ever desired for himself. When he'd learned of it, he'd been incredulous at first. And then, he'd known a moment of regret, of marrow-deep sadness that the one feat which would have made Rose want to marry him years ago had come far too late.

As for the castle, he hadn't wanted to see it. Returning to Scotland after so long away filled him with a host of mixed reactions, chief amongst them dread. He had delayed for as long as possible.

"Nay, I havenae seen it since I learned it was tae be mine," he said simply rather than divulge all that to Madeline.

"Why not?" she asked, and then her expressive face

changed. He thought he saw a flicker of hurt there before she forced a pained smile. "Never mind. You needn't tell me. I can see the answer for myself written on your countenance. It's because of *her* that you haven't been back."

Lachlan sighed. He didn't want to think about Rose any longer. Nor did he want her to become a specter who perpetually haunted his marriage with Madeline. It startled him to realize how much he cared about what his new wife thought about him. How she felt about him.

"It's no' because of her, lass," he said gently.

But the damage had already been done. Madeline was looking at him with suspicion.

"It is. Why lie to me?"

Fair enough.

"It's no' solely because of her," he amended.

Which didn't make Madeline any happier. Her lips pursed into a disapproving line. "Does she have a name, this paragon who stole your heart?"

"It doesnae matter." And he didn't want to say it aloud. It was almost as if saying Rose's name would conjure her. Make her more than just the memory that had been haunting him these many years. "And she isnae a paragon. Trust me on that."

"But you still love her." Madeline's gaze searched his.

She wasn't asking a question but making a statement. Perhaps an accusation.

"I dinnae love her any longer, lass," he reassured her, startled to realize the veracity of his words.

He still felt the same sting of betrayal when he thought of Rose. But he no longer thought about what might have been. He didn't long for her as he once had. Time and Rose's defection had cured him of that affliction.

"Are you certain?" Madeline asked, frowning.

"Aye, lass." He took one of her hands in his, raising her fingers to his lips and kissing them. "Ye're my wife."

Wife. And there was another strange word. So small, and yet it encompassed something that was larger than the both of them.

"I'm aware of that," she said pointedly, her gaze dipping to his mouth.

The urge to kiss her went from a flickering flame to a raging fire. Lachlan surrendered, lowering his head and taking her lips with his. She opened for his tongue, and he delved into the velvety recesses, tasting the sweet hints of wine she'd consumed at the wedding breakfast. He could get inebriated on her mouth alone. But he knew that he had to proceed with caution.

Lachlan raised his head with great reluctance, ending the kiss before it had truly begun. "There now. No more talk of anyone else. This is our wedding day. There shouldnae be anyone between us."

"I'm sorry to bring up the past," she said softly. "I didn't mean to dredge up unwanted feelings."

"Let's speak of other things," he suggested, thinking that he would prefer to speak about anything else.

He didn't want Rose on his mind. She didn't belong here in this moment, in this space, in this marriage. She belonged to the past, and it would be best if she remained there. He would have to see her soon enough.

"What do you wish to speak of?" Madeline asked, folding her hands primly in her lap.

"Tell me more about ye," he suggested. "About yer home in New York City."

"Our family home or the city itself?" she asked, apparently willing to be distracted.

"Yer home."

"My father built it several years ago," she said. "It's the largest home in the city. He made certain of it."

Apparently, Mr. William Chartrand's wealth and his sense of self-importance were proportionally large. Lachlan wasn't surprised. His own interactions with the man had been limited to terse telegrams, but he found himself curious about what manner of man Madeline's father was. About what her childhood had been like. About everything that concerned her, really.

"Will ye miss it?" he asked.

"I suspect so," she said, a wistful tone creeping into her voice. "But perhaps you can visit there with me one day."

"Maybe ye'll be tired of me by then and ye'll be happy tae leave me behind," he said, tamping down the tender emotions that had threatened to rise at her words.

"Or perhaps we'll become inseparable and I'll take you to show off my handsome Scottish duke to all the pretentious society ladies my mother wants to impress," she countered, her tone light.

Something inside Lachlan seized.

"Ye think me handsome, lass?" he asked, his voice husky with emotion he didn't seem capable of suppressing, regardless of how ruthlessly he longed to quash it.

She's dangerous, warned the voice inside his head. The voice he'd never listened to with Rose. The voice he most definitely should listen to with Madeline.

"Of course." A becoming flush stole over her cheeks. "Surely you know that I find you very handsome indeed by now."

"I ken ye like my kisses," he said gruffly. "And ye like when I touch ye."

He shouldn't have said that. Or thought it. He most certainly shouldn't be thinking about touching her now. *Not on the train*, he scolded himself inwardly. *Not on the damned train, ye fool.*

He would tear her out of that gown when they were safely ensconced in their hotel for the night in Edinburgh. With his teeth.

"I also happen to find you handsome," Madeline said softly. "Verra, verra handsome, if you must know."

She was teasing him, smiling in that infectious way of hers. The way that made him want to smile back and forget why he should never entrust his heart to another woman again.

"We'll make a Scot of ye yet, lass," he said lightly, as if he were entirely unaffected by her proximity, her scent, her tempting lips, the revelations she'd just made. One thing was clear. He had to get out of this car and stretch his legs. To find the wits that seemed to have been relentlessly scattered to the wind, sent out the train window into the passing scenery. He cleared his throat and rose to his feet. "Now then, can I get ye something from the refreshment car? Claret or perhaps a glass of sherry?"

"How much longer is the train ride, do you think?" she asked.

A bloody eternity.

Lachlan clenched his jaw. "Another two hours or so, I should think."

"A glass of sherry then, if you please," she said, making to rise. "I'll accompany you."

"No," he hastened to reassure her, louder than necessary, his voice echoing in the private car's handsomely appointed space. "That is tae say, ye're tired after all the excitement of the day. Ye should remain here. Let yer husband attend tae ye."

And there he went again, using that word. *Husband.* With

it came more unwanted feelings. Feelings he couldn't bear to entertain.

Lachlan didn't wait to hear Madeline's response. He fled the car as if his arse were on fire.

CHAPTER 10

With a happy sigh, Madeline toed off her favorite pair of boots, wiggling her toes and savoring the pleasure of no longer having her feet constrained tightly within the impractical footwear. When she had settled on wearing them for traveling, she hadn't taken into consideration how much walking she would need to engage in at the train stations.

"What a relief to be freed from those torture devices," she said, flexing her stockinged toes at Lachlan, who had removed his outerwear as well and was watching her from across the chamber with an inscrutable look.

He'd been as skittish as a newborn colt on the train ride, leaping to fetch her sherry and making certain to keep a polite distance between them after his return. If she didn't know better, she would have thought her new husband disliked her.

"Yer feet are sore, lass?" he asked.

"Terribly." She winced as she padded across the luxuriously thick carpet toward a chair in the sitting area of their room. "I'm afraid I only have myself to blame, however. I should have known better than to wear those boots."

He met her halfway across the room, a concerned expression on his face, and swept her into his arms without warning. Madeline gave out a small whoop of startlement, clinging to his broad shoulders. She should be accustomed to Lachlan's formidable size and strength by now, but the truth was, he was something of a gentle giant. She often forgot how tall and brawny he was until moments like this one and that day at the castle ruins when he'd single-handedly saved her life by blocking her from the falling stone wall with his body.

"I can walk," she protested breathlessly as he carried her the rest of the way to the divan she'd been intent upon occupying.

"Of course ye ken, but yer feet are aching, and ye've a husband tae carry ye now," he said smoothly. "Ye should have told me ye were in pain."

For a foolish moment, she wondered if he would carry her about thusly every day if she wore her boots. "Why, would you have carried me through the train station and the hotel?"

"Aye," he said without hesitation. "I would have gladly done so."

"I suspect that may have been the cause of some shock and surprise from our fellow travelers," she teased, smiling.

He sank into the divan, arranging Madeline so that she was comfortably seated at one end, with her feet in his lap. "I wouldnae have given a damn."

And she knew he wouldn't have. He didn't care much about what others thought of him, which was quite refreshing. He couldn't have been further from Mother and her social grasping and Charles the confidence man. Madeline was relieved.

Lachlan took her feet in his big hands and began gently pressing his thumbs into her arches. Wondrous sensation stole over her.

She couldn't stifle her moan of appreciation. "Oh, Lachlan, that's lovely. Never stop."

He chuckled, gently squeezing her sore feet. "I'll rub yer feet all night long if I must."

"I might like for you to rub elsewhere after a bit," she dared cheekily.

The look he sent in her direction was nothing short of scorching. The raw yearning in his expression made her heart beat faster. But he continued massaging her aching feet just the same, and she watched him wrestle the same desire burning within her into submission.

"My dear wife, I do believe ye're trying tae tempt me," he said with soft, deliberate intent.

She bit her lip, watching him from beneath lowered lashes, struggling with the longing that never seemed to stray far whenever she was in his presence. "Am I succeeding?"

"I'm a weak man where ye're concerned. Surely the last few weeks have proven that."

His Scots burr fell over her like a caress. She had thought that perhaps every Scottish accent would leave her so moved. However, now that they had decamped from the train and crossed paths with any number of Scots along the way, she had her answer. It was not the accent itself that affected her. It was the man. Lachlan's deep tones filled her with an ache as surely as his kisses and touch did.

She was falling deeper and deeper under her new husband's spell. And while the knowledge terrified her, Madeline was powerless to stop it.

"Actually, the last few weeks have proven the opposite," she told him, forcing herself to think of anything other than the way she felt for Lachlan. "You're a very strong man, physically and when it comes to your principles. Regimented and determined. I admire that greatly."

She admired *him*. Full stop.

"Ye best watch yer tongue, lass. I'll start tae get a heid so large it willnae fit through the doorways," he teased lightly, continuing his tender ministrations on her feet.

It felt wonderful, his hands on her, kneading the tension and pain from her aching soles. But as lovely as it was, it wasn't enough. She wanted more. Needed more. They hadn't yet dined, having only just arrived at their hotel and settling in. But it wasn't food she was hungry for just now.

"We can't have that, can we?" she asked, and then she slid her feet from his lap and went to stand before him, presenting him with her back. "Will you assist me? I find I'd like to be freed of some of my layers for a spell."

"Of course." His voice was husky and deep, laden with desire.

She felt the light touch of his fingers skimming over fastenings, her bodice beginning to loosen and gape as he made his way down the long row of pearls. When the last button came free of its mooring, she shrugged the garment from her shoulders. The tapes of her skirt came next, untied to send them falling to the floor in a lush pool of silk. Meticulously, he undressed her, laces opening, hooks and eyes coming apart, silk and petticoats and satin giving way until she was clad in nothing more than her chemise and stockings.

Madeline turned toward him at last. Lachlan was still seated on the divan, looking like a giant perched on a piece of dollhouse furniture. His blue eyes burned into her, his large hands resting on his muscled thighs, his long legs indolently splayed before him. She stepped into the vee, drawn to him as ever.

"Are ye more comfortable now, lass?" he asked, his gaze

trailing over her form in a way that made her nipples go hard.

"Not yet," she said and then settled on his lap astride him, her chemise riding up her thighs as she draped her arms around his neck. "This is an improvement, however."

"Aye." His eyes were on her mouth now, hungry and hot, his hands clamping on her waist. "Quite an improvement."

"It could be better," she said and then brought her lips to his.

She had intended to seduce him. To woo him. To turn this big man to putty in her hands. But the moment her mouth was on his, Lachlan took command of the kiss. He cupped her nape, and his tongue glided into her open mouth like a declaration that she was his. And she *was* his. She hadn't felt it, not so precisely, until this moment, straddling him on a hotel divan, the evidence of his desire for her rising to rigid prominence against her aching sex.

She kissed him with every ounce of desire she had, all the emotion, all the yearning, all the newfound wonder. Her fingers sifted through his soft, too-long hair, and she pressed herself nearer to him, until her breasts strained against his chest, wishing that she could be closer still. That she could somehow be cleaved to him, a part of him that would never leave.

The intensity of her emotions astounded her. Everything was Lachlan. The heady scent of him, soap and fir, the rippling strength of his corded muscles. The low groan she happily swallowed up. The hand on the small of her back, holding her to him, the fingers gently grazing the sensitive skin of her neck, the drugging play of his lips over hers. Her surroundings had become a heady blur, and she willingly surrendered herself to the burning desire that made her nipples hard and her sex throb. He had resisted taking her for weeks, and she wanted to give herself to him.

Now.

She wanted to tear down the remnants of his past and set fire to them. Wanted to love him so well that he would no longer remember the woman he'd loved, the one who had so wounded him that he had vowed to never again allow himself to be vulnerable. She wanted to erase the pain he'd suffered. She wanted to be his wife in more than name.

His lips left hers to trail in reverent adoration along the column of her throat.

"Lass," he murmured. "I cannae promise tae be regimented now. If we dinnae stop…"

As if he couldn't force his mind to complete the sentence, his words trailed away, and his mouth traveled over her bare skin, sending hot sparks of desire skittering over her in his wake. She grasped handfuls of his hair, holding him to her as he feasted on her throat.

"I don't want to stop," she murmured.

His hands moved, traveling lower until he clasped her bottom through her chemise, his fingers sinking into her willing flesh with possessive demand. "Ye undo me."

She might have said the same to him, but then Lachlan dragged more openmouthed kisses along her collarbone, robbing her of speech and thought. She was nothing but an aching, longing, lustful lump of clay in the hands of a master, being turned into something extraordinary. He found her nipple through the fine fabric of her chemise and sucked hard. Madeline writhed against him, the friction of his fabric-covered cock on her aching flesh making her nearly out of her mind.

She wanted her chemise gone. She wanted his garments on the floor. She wanted to be naked with him. She wanted his cock in her mouth. It was a pleasure she hadn't expected to enjoy so much, and she had greedily seized every opportunity she'd had to do so in stolen, furtive moments because she loved to please him and watch him become helpless but to surrender to her, even if his conscience dictated the opposite.

Captivated by the idea that she would please him again now, she disengaged from Lachlan, scooting off his lap. She sank to her knees before him and reached for the fastening on the fall of his trousers.

"By all that's holy, lass," he hissed, his voice tight with lust, his jaw taut. "What are ye doing?"

Buttons popped open with ease. She had acquainted herself with his clothing and his body quite well these last few weeks. She knew how to divest him of his garments with remarkable alacrity, just as she knew how to drive him wild with need. She parted the placket in his smalls, and his cock sprang free, massive and thick and beautiful. She loved this part of him, soft and yet hard, capable of bringing him so much pleasure, deliciously sensitive to the touch while the rest of him remained strong and implacable.

"I want you in my mouth," she told him, and then, without waiting for his honorable protests to the contrary, she lowered her head and took him deep into her throat, as far as she could without gagging.

There was an art to the act, and she had begun to learn it with practice. As always, the thick glide of him in her mouth made her inner muscles clench, desire pooling between her thighs. She licked and sucked, applying herself to the task with careful determination, using her hand and her mouth on him until he was groaning above her, his hand slipping into her still-upswept hair, his hips moving restlessly beneath her.

She withdrew to the tip, holding him in a firm grip as she laved the head of his cock with her tongue, taking care to hold his gaze as she lavished him with attention. His eyes

were dark with lust. He'd never looked more beautiful to her
—all his powerful strength at her mercy.

He was hers.

Madeline licked up the bead of moisture seeping from the
small slit, stroking him as the taste of him filled her with
more fire. Words spilled from his lips in a stream from
above. Her name. Tender words. Words she didn't
understand.

"Madeline, *mo gràidh*. Ye have tae stop or I'll no' make it."

She smiled around his thick length, pleased to see him so
flushed and hungry for her, to know she was able to give him
pleasure. But her determination to make him completely lose
control was thwarted by his own. He gently disengaged from
her, tucking himself back into his trousers, before standing.
He drew her to her feet, his trousers low on his hips, and
took her into his arms before carrying her across the room
to the high tester bed. With calm, efficient motions, he
stripped away her chemise, along with her drawers and
stockings. He shrugged out of his own garments as she
watched, naked and reclining on the bed.

When he joined her, she reached for him, but he wasn't
finished with his task. Lachlan kissed and teased his way up
her bare legs, lingering on her knees and inner thighs before
he parted them. Cool air washed over her intimate flesh,
bared to his heated gaze.

"*Bòidheach*," he proclaimed, another word that was unfamiliar to her.

But then his tongue flicked over her center, and she
forgot to wonder at the meaning. Instead, she surrendered to
his mouth on her. He found her clitoris and sucked, making
her hips buck. Attending to him had made her desperately
ready. She was wet and aching, and when he applied himself
to her pleasure, Lachlan had her perilously near to finding
her release already.

As he lapped at her, he sank a finger inside her sheath, the invasion making her tip her hips in welcome. He slid deeper, adding a second finger, stretching her, finding a place so sensitive that it seemed a miraculous secret only he could unlock. The first wave of release hit her like a bolt of lightning streaking through a summer sky—sudden and awe-inspiring. She came apart with complete disregard for the throaty moans emerging from her, grasping handfuls of bedclothes and arching into his handsome face. The addition of the slight abrasion of his teeth made her see stars. She cried out as more waves of delight shimmered through her, making her feel boneless and weightless.

How good it felt, and yet as wondrous as it was, she wanted more.

Lachlan understood what she needed. What they both needed. He rose over her, his powerful, massive body cloaking hers with heat and strength. He dotted worshipful kisses over her belly and breasts on his way to her mouth. And then he kissed her, his lips wet with her own desire, the taste of her mingling with the taste of him on her tongue. It was the purest commingling—the two of them coming together as he pressed his cock to her entrance.

He was large, so much larger than his fingers.

She thought of how huge he was when fully erect and wondered how she could fit that part of him inside her. He would stretch her until she broke apart, it seemed. But she wasn't fearful. Lachlan would protect her and treat her tenderly as he always did. She had unquestioning faith in this man, her husband and, soon, her lover.

The pressure began to build. Lachlan kissed a path to her ear. "Are ye ready, *mo gràidh?*"

"Yes," she gasped out, restless under him, until she thought past her selfish, greedy desires. "Are you sure? Your vow…"

She didn't want him to regret this. To regret her. And despite all that had happened between them thus far, all they had shared, she needed him to be utterly certain.

"My vow is tae ye now," he said, kissing her ear, her cheek.

Such reverence. For her. He made her feel as if she were precious to him.

Beloved.

But that was a foolish fancy she mustn't entertain. Even if he surrendered to the passion flaring between them, she mustn't forget that this was a marriage of convenience. He had saved her from a marriage of Father's choosing, and she was saving his castle from ruin.

He moved, thrusting, joining with her, chasing away the unwanted thoughts crowding her mind. She forgot to think and instead turned herself over to sensation. He guided her legs around his waist, opening her to him, and the new angle provided the perfect means for him to slide deeper. It was exquisite. It was pain and pleasure all at once.

"How are ye, lass?" he wanted to know, his tone solicitous but strained.

Almost as if it aggrieved him to proceed so slowly.

"More," she said raggedly. "Give me more of you."

With a growl, he surged again, then again, until he was fully seated inside her, lodged so deep, the pleasure and sting of his possession bringing tears to her eyes. She blinked them away, and he stiffened above her, raising his head to look down, a troubled expression on his face.

"Have I hurt ye?"

He sounded horrified at the prospect.

She cupped his face in her hands. "Never. You could never hurt me."

But that wasn't true, was it? A sudden, painful realization struck her as her new husband kissed away the stray tear that had escaped the corner of her eye. He *could* hurt her, but not in the physical sense. It wasn't his large body and brute strength that she feared. It was her own heart, which seemed to beat for this man alone.

Whilst his had only ever beaten for another.

"I'll try tae go slowly, lass," he promised, kissing her cheek, her jaw, then lower. Down her throat until he took one of her nipples into his hot mouth.

He sucked as he began to move within her. The glide of his thickness inside her had Madeline crying out in wonder. Nothing could have prepared her for this. For him. The books failed to describe it; they were but a pale, rudimentary attempt at conveying the all-encompassing miracle of Lachlan making love to her. Slowly, with such tenderness and care, making no demands of her but only stoking the fires ever higher.

His mouth fastened on her other breast, and he slowly withdrew from her, only to sink deep inside again. All the while, desire coiled tightly within her. Tighter and tighter like a watch spring. Her hands traveled over him, moving over the bare expanse of his muscled back, over his chest. Along his arms, absorbing the flex and strength.

His lips found their way back to hers, and he kissed her deeply, giving her his tongue as he plunged into her with his cock, taking her faster and harder, some of the gentleness fading away as their mutual passions burned hotter. She clung to him, gasping out her pleasure into his mouth, and he drank up each breathy moan as if it were an elixir, his lips moving over hers as his body moved inside her.

And then there was a new sensation. His fingers were somehow between their bodies, at the place where they were joined, brushing over the bud of her sex in firm, commanding strokes that coaxed a new climax from her with scarcely any effort. She shattered beneath him, raking her nails down his back. Sheer bliss washed over her as she tightened on his length, drawing him deep as if even her body conspired to hold him there forever, the prisoner of her mad lust.

"Lass," he murmured against her lips, moving against her in more frenzied thrusts now, a sheen of sweat coating his skin. "I'm trying tae make this last, but ye feel so good wrapped around me. So tight and hot and wet. Like paradise."

That was how he felt too. Paradise in her arms, inside her. She never wanted to leave this bed. She never wanted to dress. No, she would remain here with him, naked and wanton, exploring his body every way she could.

"Yes," she cried out, scraping her nails up and down his broad back.

Her actions seemed to spur him on, because he moved faster, harder. Thrusting into her with tight, measured strokes that threatened to send her over the edge yet again. He tore his mouth from hers and rose above her, majestic and handsome, like some conqueror of old claiming her as forever his. He pumped into her twice more, the cords of his neck going taut, his eyes closing. He was beautiful in his release. Beautiful in the way he planted himself deep.

She was going to come again. It was wonderful, a golden haze filling her mind. She watched him, his body moving in fluid motions. Another tremor tore through Madeline, and then she knew the hot rush of his seed filling her. Lachlan collapsed atop her, holding her to him tightly, his breathing as ragged as hers, his heart pounding fiercely against her breast.

She held him to her, an astonishing realization hitting her in that moment as the languorous lull of sated desire licked through her. She had never felt as if she belonged somewhere more than when she was in this man's arms.

CHAPTER 11

*L*achlan watched Madeline sleep.

Some time ago, the tray of sustenance he'd rung for had been delivered. It was likely cold by now. But despite his ravenous appetite, he wasn't moved to eat or leave her side, apart from accepting the tray, which had been a necessary obligation. She'd slept through the light commotion, never waking, apparently exhausted by the combination of wedding day, train travel, and lovemaking.

They had taken an early meal prior to arriving at the station in York to depart for Edinburgh. The train they caught had stopped for half an hour in York, having arrived from London. That had all been hours ago, what may as well have been a lifetime for the changes those hours had wrought. And by now, he was starving, his stomach grumbling loudly in demanding protest.

And yet, he remained where he was, listening to the rhythmic sound of her breathing, drinking in the sight of her, lovely and at ease, her chestnut hair spread over the pillow. She was beautiful. And his. His to love, to kiss, to hold. To protect, to make love to, to make a life with.

What an arresting realization. It was settling in now, their change in circumstance, becoming real in the wake of their earlier lovemaking. Everything was different. *He* was different too. Lachlan didn't yet know what it all meant. Part of him was too fearful to investigate.

Because he could see now, with utter and abject clarity, how easy it would be for him to fall in love again. Specifically, to fall in love with Madeline. His bold and vibrant American spitfire, who was brazen and confident in every action she took. Who seized what she wanted, when she wanted it, without apology. Who was spirited and determined and stubborn and intelligent.

How he hoped she didn't regret her decision to marry him, because it occurred to him that marrying Madeline had easily been the best thing he had ever done. Not because of the fortune that came along with her, but because of the woman herself. He couldn't fathom his life without her in it. And suddenly, he knew, in some small measure, what Decker must have been speaking of when he had extolled the virtues of love and marriage that day at the fountain at Sherborne Manor.

As if roused by the heavy nature of his thoughts, Madeline shifted and stretched, making a sleepy, kittenish sound that sent a pang of something directly to his heart. She was smiling as her eyes fluttered open, and then his heart did something else. It cracked open.

At least, that was how it felt.

She stole his breath.

"Hullo," she told him softly.

"Hullo, *mo gràidh.*"

The endearment came naturally. This, too, was cause for concern. He didn't like how strong his feelings for Madeline were, and yet he was also powerless to stop them. They were a train, speeding down a track, determined to reach their inevitable destination.

"Mo gràidh," she repeated. "What does it mean?"

My love.

But he couldn't bring himself to say those words in English. Not yet. It was too soon, and he was caught in the maelstrom of his burgeoning emotions.

"It's a Scottish word for wife," he fibbed.

Her brow furrowed. "Is there a Scottish word for husband, then?"

Damn. He ought to have known better than to lie to her. But he hadn't been prepared to make such an admission. Not to her, nor to himself. Because he very much feared that he had fallen in love with her, and although she was now his wife and he needn't worry about her choosing someone else over him in a matrimonial sense, he was more than aware of how new their relationship was. She could grow bored with him. Displeased with him. She could decide that lumbering, red-haired Scotsmen with ramshackle castles had lost their dubious appeal. She could long to return to New York City or even London. She could come to resent and despise him for their sudden marriage.

"Aye," he told her grimly. "It's husband."

"But how odd," she said, her nose crinkling in an adorable way as she considered his stupid lie. "Why would there be such a lovely word for wife and not one for husband?"

"Because husbands dinnae deserve either our wives or a lovely name." He leaned toward her, kissing her to keep her sharp mind from turning the question over and reaching the inevitable conclusion—that he was a dunderheaded clodpoll.

She wrapped her arms around his neck, her lips clinging to his, her soft curves melting into his frame. His cock sprang to attention, rising proudly and prominently between them.

Madeline tipped her head back, ending the kiss with an

impish grin, her eyes dancing. "Did you miss me while I slept?"

Her teasing voice only heightened his unfortunate state.

"Of course I missed ye," he growled affectionately, dropping a kiss on the bridge of her elegant nose. "But ye earned that slumber after the day ye've had."

"What about you?" She ran her fingers lightly through his hair, the fondness on her countenance as unmistakable as it was heady. "Did you not sleep?"

"I dozed for a bit," he said, and then his stupid stomach promptly grumbled.

Madeline's brows rose. "It sounds as if you've worked up an appetite."

"Aye, I have." A twofold appetite. But one would have to wait. He didn't wish to fall upon poor Madeline like a slavering beast.

It wasn't her fault that he had been chaste as a monk for years and that now that he'd had his first taste of lovemaking with her, more was all he could think about. His prick was a damned demanding fellow, but he could exercise some patience.

"How long have I been asleep?" she fretted. "I don't suppose we can procure a meal now."

"I rang for a tray whilst ye were asleep," he said. "Are ye hungry?"

"I could be." She smiled shyly.

And by the rood, that smile went straight to his cock. He tried to think of kittens to make the bastard wilt.

"I'll make up a plate for ye," he offered, thinking the distraction would be excellent and also that he wanted to dote on her.

To take care of her. To spoil her. To cherish her too.

Aye, he was a fool for this woman already. The rest of his life didn't bode particularly well if he was desperately in love on the first day of their marriage. How would he be able to remain impervious?

He slid from the bed before she could answer and strode across the room, bare arsed. He'd never possessed much shame, and he knew Madeline enjoyed his body. He often caught her admiring his form, and it pleased him greatly.

"You needn't serve me," she protested languidly from the bed. "I'm fully capable of tending to myself."

"Aye, but as I told ye before, ye have me now, lass," he reminded her, pouring two glasses of wine, one for each of them, before examining the contents of the covered tray.

Fresh bread and cheese, along with tongue and cold roast beef. Best of all, there were shortbreads. A divine feast as far as he was concerned, but then he was so hungry, he would have happily eaten his own hat at this point. Lachlan made haste in filling plates for each of them, making two trips to deliver her wine and overflowing plate, before returning with his own and settling back in the bed.

"I can say with all honesty that I've never been served in bed by a naked man before," Madeline said teasingly when he was settled at her side once more. "If this is what being married entails, I shouldn't have waited."

"But if ye hadnae waited, ye wouldnae have married me," he pointed out, raising his wine in her direction. "And I, for one, am heartily glad I'm the lucky one ye married."

She raised her glass as well, giving him a tender look that melted the last remaining bit of ice within him. "I'm glad too."

"Ye are?" He cast a glance in her direction, shortbread halfway to his mouth. "Truly?"

"Do you doubt it? If so, I must be remiss in my duties as wife. I'll have to make amends."

Good Christ above, if she were any more thorough in her duties as his wife, she'd kill him.

He bit into his shortbread, enjoying the flavor of it, considering his words with care as he chewed and swallowed. "Ye've proven an excellent wife thus far. No need tae make amends."

"I've only been a wife for the span of mere hours," she said, a playful grin flirting with the corners of her lips. "How can I have already passed muster?"

The admission was torn from him. "Because ye make me happy, lass."

He knew he shouldn't have said it. But he couldn't seem to help himself where she was concerned.

"Thank you," she said softly, looking at him in a way he couldn't recall another woman ever doing before her. "You make me happy too, Lachlan."

He stuffed another shortbread into his mouth to keep from saying anything else, and they carried on with their repast in companionable silence.

"I'LL MISS IT HERE," Madeline declared as she took another lingering look out the window of their hotel, which was across from the Scott Monument and down the street from the beautiful Princes Street Gardens and the castle atop its perch on Castle Rock. She and Lachlan had toured both during their sojourn in Edinburgh.

They had remained for longer than originally planned, Lachlan needing to take care of matters concerning the estate and entail, the details of which had required more time than he had supposed. But they had also turned their stay in the city into a honeymoon of sorts.

She and Lachlan had been luxuriating in their time alone together, alternating between making love and touring the city, Madeline eagerly taking in the rich history and sights.

Edinburgh was so much older than New York City, and she and Lachlan had enjoyed visiting confectioneries and filling themselves with shortbreads and Scottish cakes, paying a visit to the Royal Institution with its Antiquarian Museum, the National Gallery and its collection of paintings and statues. It had been a whirlwind.

And now, it was nearly at an end.

There was yet another leg of their journey remaining—the final one to Kenross Castle, south and east of the city. They'd be leaving in two days and traveling by carriage to visit the sprawling, if dilapidated, estate and ascertain how much work would need to be completed at Castle Kenross to restore it to its former glory. And with that impending expedition loomed a question she had yet to ask but that had been eating away at her like a gnawing little kitchen mouse just the same.

"We can always return for another visit," Lachlan said as he approached her from behind and wrapped his arms around her waist, burying his face in her neck and inhaling deeply, as if he couldn't get enough of her scent.

"Perhaps when we return to England for Lucy's wedding," Madeline said wistfully, watching the horses and carriages and crush of people moving about their days below.

"Aye, whenever ye wish." He kissed a deceptively sensitive place just behind her ear, a spot that never failed to make her knees go weak.

Madeline settled her arms over his, hugging him to her more tightly, the heat and strength of him at her back a welcome temptation she could never seem to resist. How good she felt in his arms. Safe. Protected. Adored.

Not loved, but she harbored some hope that, in time, the affection Lachlan felt for her would evolve into something more pronounced. Something like what she was feeling for him. Because it was as plain as the nose on her face that she had somehow, over the course of the last few weeks, fallen helplessly, hopelessly in love with her husband.

She watched the progression of a stately carriage below, gathering the courage to formulate the question she needed to ask. "You told me that you left Scotland and the life you knew behind, that you found your position with Mr. Decker. But you never did say if you'd returned to Scotland for a visit. Surely you must have come back in all the time you were gone. You must have missed your home."

What she truly wanted to know was if he had been so devastated by what had unfolded with the woman he'd loved that he hadn't had the heart to return.

There was silence for a moment, and she feared he wouldn't answer her. He nuzzled her temple instead, the arms wrapped around her waist tightening incrementally. Until at last, he spoke.

"I didnae return."

Simple words, and yet they held so much meaning.

"Why?" she asked as the carriage she'd been particularly watching turned a corner and disappeared from sight.

"Because I didnae wish tae," he said gruffly.

"Do you not have family here?" she asked, turning to cast him a sidelong glance. "Friends you must have missed?"

"The only family I cared for was my mother, and without her, there was no' a reason tae return. Until obligation and duty changed that. As I said, I dinnae expect tae inherit the title. I'm a distant cousin of a distant cousin."

That answered part of her question, but something remained unspoken between them. There was the woman whose name he hadn't even deigned to tell her. The woman who had so captivated him. Jealousy rose unwanted within her, curdling the delicious shortbread she'd taken earlier with her tea.

She sighed, hesitant to bring up the past again. Their idyll had been everything she could have hoped for—she was enjoying his company, his lovemaking, his sense of adventure. She was far happier than she had dreamed she would be in a marriage of convenience with a stranger she'd known for the span of less than two months.

"There's something ye're no' saying," he observed knowingly, his bright eyes made more vibrant by the sun pouring through the window, the gilded rays catching the golds in his hair and bringing them to life. He hadn't shaved that morning, for they'd been lazy and stayed abed far longer than they should have, alternately making love and napping. The light caught in the faint stubble that kissed his jaw.

She knew how that stubble felt, coarse and wonderful, on her inner thighs. On her breasts and neck. She knew so much about him—the intimate, the physical. She knew how to make him moan. How to take off his clothing. He'd even shown her how to shave him, a tender task she'd taken delight in performing for him the morning before. She knew that he adored lettuce and tangy vinaigrettes. That shortbreads were his secret weakness. And that he tended to slam every door he closed on his own, as if he were oblivious to his strength. She knew the sound of his breathing when he slept. Knew the scent of him in the secret place where she loved to burrow her face, between his neck and shoulder.

But there remained so much of him that was an enigma.

And there was a part of him that he kept deliberately separate, locked away with a key only he possessed.

"What's troubling ye, lass?" he pressed when she failed to answer him, caught up in her thoughts.

Madeline had to turn away from the stirring sight of his handsome face and sky-blue eyes. She returned her gaze to the city street bustling with life instead, choosing her next words with care.

"The woman you loved," she began at last. "Is she the reason you stayed away?"

"Lass," he protested softly, kissing the shell of her ear. "Ye dinnae need tae fret about the past."

His words did nothing to mollify her concern.

"You didn't answer me," she pointed out, fearing that he'd said everything by saying nothing at all.

"Aye, then. If ye must hear it, she's the reason I didnae return initially. But look at me, *mo gràidh.*"

There it was again. The word for wife that rolled so fluently off his tongue. She still found it strange that there was no equivalent for husband.

Madeline complied, turning to face him so that her back was against the cool windowpane, no longer looking out at the world, but instead looking in, to the sight of her husband dressed informally in nothing but a shirt, trousers, and bare feet. His feet were enormous, like the rest of him, but they were handsome feet. She'd never seen a man so well-formed on such a grand scale.

"I've lived a full life these last few years," he said softly, a tenderness overtaking his features that she'd come to recognize. "Or at least, I thought I had. Until I met ye. Now, I'm persuaded I was wrong and that I was missing something verra, verra important."

She wanted to believe him. Her foolish heart leapt.

"Oh? And what were you missing that was so important?" she asked, feigning ignorance.

He caught her in a loose embrace, pulling her into his chest. "Ye, of course. Ye're what I've been missing all along, and now that I've found ye, I'll no' be letting ye go. So please, dinnae worry over what happened in the past. I'm looking tae the future now. Tae the life we'll build."

It was difficult to sweep away the jealousy that lingered whenever she thought about the mysterious lover from his past. The woman who had owned his heart. Harder still not to feel envious. But he was right. There was no need to worry about a woman he hadn't seen in years. Whoever she was, she was nothing but a memory. Madeline wouldn't allow her to eclipse the growing feelings she had for her husband or to taint the brightness of the future awaiting them.

No, she would chase the ghosts of the past. Kiss by kiss, touch by touch. She would make him forget. And suddenly, she knew the way to do it.

She cupped his nape and rose on her toes, aligning her lips to his. The kiss was slow and ardent, rife with unspoken meaning, burning with potent lust. She had never wanted him more, and whether it was to solidify her claim on him or to continue chipping away at the armor he wore about his heart, she couldn't say. All she knew was that she had to have him inside her. She had to have him naked, atop her, entwined with her.

She gave him her tongue, showing him without words what she sought. And with a half groan, half growl, he accepted her offering, his tongue mating with hers until they were both breathless and her breasts were heavy and full, her nipples tightened to painful points, her sex aching.

Madeline was first to break the kiss, brushing her lower lip over his just one more time before she spoke, unable to get enough. "Please, Lachlan. I need you."

He cursed in Gaelic, words she didn't understand. "What ye do tae me, lass."

She wanted to do more.

Everything.

Wanted to drive the memories of the woman he'd lost from his mind forever so that only Madeline remained.

She slid her hand boldly over the front of his trousers,

where his cock had already risen to rigid prominence. "I feel what I do to you. And I like it very much."

She gave him a slow stroke, her hand firm and knowing. Touching him made her long to feel all that hardness inside her, filling her, taking her.

"The bed," he growled. "Now."

They staggered toward the piece of furniture in question together, pulling off each other's garments as they went. Her bodice landed on a chair. Her drawers sailed across a table. His waistcoat nearly landed in the fire grate. Thankfully, the fire was out.

They kissed frantically as their fingers traveled over buttons and cloth, the sound of rending fabric filling the air when it took too long to remove her chemise and Lachlan tore off one sleeve in his urgency. At last, he was as naked as she, and they were on the bed, Lachlan atop her, his powerful body pinning hers to the bed, his cock springing huge and demanding against her sex.

She rubbed herself against him, seeking the friction of his erection over her clitoris, and he lowered his head to suck the tip of one breast into his hot, wet mouth. She moaned, feeling how ready she was for him, how desperate. His hand slipped between her legs, petting her lightly in a bold tease of what she craved.

"More," she begged shamelessly. "Please, Lachlan. Give me more."

He released her nipple and swirled his tongue lazily around the distended peak. "How much more?"

He traced her seam, painting her folds with her own wetness while keeping his touch maddeningly light.

"Not enough," she said, her hips moving, seeking.

He cupped her mound, rubbing with excruciating gentleness, somehow avoiding the place where she wanted him most. "How's this, lass?"

He blew a stream of hot air over her other nipple, then sucked long and hard, the hand between her legs working her slowly into a frenzy.

"More," she repeated, nearly out of her mind with need.

Until it occurred to her that two could play at this game of wicked teasing. She knew what he liked. Madeline twisted, grasping his ruddy cock in her hand and caressing him from base to tip.

"Minx," he said without heat, at last parting her folds and giving the bud of her sex a light stroke with his fingertip.

She continued her caress, gripping him harder, stroking him faster. A drop of moisture beaded on the head of his cock, and she used her thumb to swirl it over him. He groaned, thrusting into her touch, and increased his pressure on her aching pearl.

"Come for me, lass," he murmured, kissing the curve of her breast, his wicked fingers finally giving her everything she wanted, moving fast and sure over her slick pearl.

She was helpless to stop the climax that roared through her. Crying out with her pleasure, she surrendered to the waves of bliss as everything within her tightened to the point of decadent pleasure and her cunny contracted with a series of spasms that stole her breath. Empty. She was so empty. That part of her needed to be filled.

She guided his cock to her entrance, knowing how wet she was for him. More than ready.

"Ah, *mo gràidh*." He laved her nipple with his tongue one more time before moving back to her lips, taking them in a fierce, claiming kiss. "Ye're soaked for me. So hot and wet and perfect."

Madeline hitched her leg over his hips, opening herself to him in silent invitation. And he took what she offered, thrusting into her in one long stroke that had them gasping in unison. He was buried deep inside her, and the pleasure was so exquisite, she thought for a wild moment that she might die of it. And that it wouldn't matter. She would shatter to pieces in his arms, and she wouldn't regret it for a moment.

But then he moved, withdrawing almost completely, only to sink deep again. So deep. Finding the rhythm they both needed. And she forgot to think. Forgot to worry about anything but Lachlan, his big body laboring over hers, his cock thrusting in and out as she reached her crescendo again. It was close. So close.

He shifted and withdrew suddenly, guiding her legs along his chest, until her feet were over his shoulders. Slowly, he folded her body, entering her again from this new position.

And she was lost.

He plunged into her, the sensation even better than before, as if he were reaching a new place inside her. Deeper. More intense. A helpless sound of desire tore from her as she clung to him, caressing his chest, his shoulders, his muscled arms, while he worked his cock in and out of her ever-sensitive sheath. His eyes, blue and intense and searing, held hers captive as he took possession of her body.

She couldn't hold on to her control. Something inside her snapped. Broke open. She came in a torrent, tightening on his cock and calling out his name as he increased his pace and thrust into her again and again, his strokes growing shorter as he sought his own release.

Until, with a hoarse cry, he emptied himself inside her, filling her with the hot flood of his seed as she pulsed around him.

He withdrew from her and lowered her legs, then took her into his arms, holding her tightly as their hearts pounded in frantic unison and their ragged breathing slowly returned to normal. Wrapped in his warmth and strength, Madeline had no doubt.

The past was firmly where it belonged.

CHAPTER 12

*I*f Lachlan had learned anything, it was that fortune was fickle, and just when it handed him a good turn on the wheel, the bad turn was coming. In this case, the bad arrived in the form of a petite, tawny-haired, blue-eyed ghost from his past.

Nay.

To be fair and precise, it had initially arrived in the form of a missive bearing familiar flourishes he could have seen in his sleep for all the times he'd read love notes written to himself in that fair hand. And aye, he was ashamed to admit he'd kept some of them, rereading them in his darkest days before pitching the lot of them into the fire and watching them burn. This missive, unlike the others, hadn't been turned to ash. It was crisp and clean and scented with perfume he'd once thought intoxicating but now found strangely cloying as it wafted from the paper to wrap itself around him.

Dearest Lachlan,

For so many years, I've longed for your return. Imagine my surprise at learning the new Duke of Kenross is here in Edinburgh at long last and that he is, in fact, you. Words cannot convey how deeply I have regretted what passed between us long ago. In my foolish youth, my heart was ruled by fear that only time and experience has banished. It is to my everlasting sorrow that I learned my lesson too late.

It's my fondest hope that you would meet with me at your earliest convenience so that I may make my apology to you directly rather than via the exceedingly insufficient means of pen and ink.

Please know that I've kept you near to my heart since we parted and dreamed of the day when we would meet once more as friends.

Ever and fondly yours,
Rose, Countess of Kelley

HIS FIRST THOUGHT, upon reading the final line of the letter, had been that the old Earl of Kelley must have died, leaving her husband to inherit the title and making Rose a countess in her own right. His second thought had been to wonder if he would have received such a loving note from Rose if he had returned to Edinburgh as Mr. Lachlan Macfie instead of the Duke of Kenross. His third thought had been to instantly send a return missive—a resounding denial of her request.

The original missive had arrived while Madeline was asleep, hand-delivered to Lachlan by one of the hotel porters. He'd felt instantly guilty as he paced the room while she slumbered, innocently unaware of the storm brewing within him. Receiving the missive from Rose felt akin to a betrayal. Responding had felt wrong. And yet, what choice had he? None —he wanted Rose to leave him alone, and he'd made that clear.

Within half an hour's time, however, it was apparent that Rose had either mistaken the intent of his answering note, or she was unwilling to accept his refusal. A porter had returned, indicating there was a guest awaiting Lachlan below in the lobby. One who was most insistent that she await him. He'd known instantly who it was. Grimly, he had thanked the porter and informed him he would be below directly.

By that time, Madeline was beginning to stir, no doubt roused from her sound slumber by the knocks at the door and Lachlan's ceaseless pacing. He'd gone to her, kissed her softly, and told her that he had some unexpected business to attend to, but that he would return forthwith.

"I'll come with you," she had protested sleepily, the bedclothes sagging to reveal her luscious breasts and berry-pink nipples.

Her hair had been unbound and streaming down her back in riotous waves as it did whenever she bathed and then allowed it to dry free of the encumbrance of a plait or chignon. He found its wildness charming; she found it exasperating. And Lachlan had wanted nothing more in the world than to climb into that bed beside her and make love to her again until everyone and everything else ceased to exist.

He smoothed a stray tendril of hair from her silken cheek instead, admiring how deliciously rumpled and well-fucked she looked and trying to quell his rampant cock, who, as usual, had a mind of his own. "I'll be back in a trice. Ye neednae concern yerself with it. The matter is a trifling one. Ye should relax before we have tae leave for Castle Kenross later this afternoon."

She'd turned her head and pressed a hot little kiss to his palm that did nothing to persuade his prick that Lachlan

175

wasn't going to shuck his trousers and join his beautiful wife in bed. "But I don't want to be here without you."

Her protest had filled him with warmth. He took her lips in a slow, lingering kiss before forcing himself to withdraw and straighten away from her, lest he remain. He needed to meet with Rose and put an end to her desire to seek him out. And the sooner he did so, the better, for he had no intention of allowing her to interfere in his new marriage.

"I'll only be gone for a scant few minutes," he promised. "In the time it'll take ye tae gather up yer gown and under-pinnings, I'll already be back at yer side where I belong."

She'd made the sleepy sound he adored and snuggled back into the bedclothes, looking like a goddess he longed to worship. And *would* worship. Just as soon as he completed this lingering business with Rose and returned to her.

"The bed is quite comfortable," Madeline had said, smiling from her pillow. "Hurry back, husband."

He'd stolen one last, lingering look at her, promising, "I will."

And now, he was standing with the woman he'd once loved in a small salon, all the better for circumspection. The clever hotel clerk had seen to their privacy; Lachlan wouldn't have thought of such a thing. But like it or not, he was the Duke of Kenross now, and he had a duchess to protect from wagging tongues and painful gossip.

Rose was as he had recalled and yet more elegant and refined than when he had known her. No doubt, she was dressed the part of the countess, wearing a gown of formidable navy silk that set off her golden hair and her sky-blue eyes to perfection. But she wore her hair as she always had, in high curls piled at her crown, tiny blue silk flowers that matched her gown tucked into the elaborate coiffure. She still looked like a fairy, her stature small—he'd been able to carry her about as if she weighed no more than a bird. But now, he rather found he preferred the long, lissome legs of his wife.

"Lachlan," Rose greeted him warmly.

Too warmly.

He offered her a curt bow. "Lady Kelley."

"Ye called me Rose once," she said, regarding him solemnly as she moved toward him.

"I called ye a great many things once," he said wryly, refraining from adding that some of those names hadn't been polite or kind.

"Ye're angry with me," she said, stopping before him, her perfume making his nose itch.

She was lovely as ever, scarcely any change in her, save the airs she possessed, the jewels at her throat and hanging from her ears, and the faint hint of lines at the corners of her lively eyes. He stared at her, trying to summon up even the faintest hint of emotion for her.

And couldn't.

There was simply...nothing. Not anger. Certainly not love. Not resentment. Not sadness. Not regret.

"I was angry with ye," he corrected. "But that was a long time ago."

He'd been devastated, in truth. It was almost impossible to believe how thoroughly destroyed he had been by her defection.

"I'm thrilled ye're no longer angry," she said, smiling at him in the way that once would have made his heart leap and had him desperate to kiss her. "I feared that was why ye refused tae see me, that ye hated me for what I'd done."

"Hate is a strong word, my lady," Lachlan said. "Ye left me brokenhearted tae be sure, but in the end, I'm in yer debt for making the decision ye did."

He read the startlement on her expressive face; that much hadn't changed. He could see what she was feeling without her saying a word. He recalled how mournful she had looked on the day she had come to him, making love with him a final time before saying her farewell. He had sensed something different about her then, but he'd been too caught up in his mad lust and love for her to question it until she had shocked him by revealing she intended to wed another.

I've made my decision, and I'll be marrying George, she'd said after she'd finished dressing herself and restoring her hair. *This is the last time we can see each other this way.*

Rose had been a young widow when they had first met in Edinburgh. She'd been clever and charming, and despite his obvious lack of genteel polish and his massive form compared to her diminutive one, she'd hung on his every word. She'd asked him to become her lover. He'd begged her to be his wife.

He ought to have understood what she had truly meant when she'd said that she couldn't marry again so soon after her first husband's death, that it would be unseemly. She'd meant that she was looking to marry a proper lordling, not someone like Lachlan. That she'd had her heart set upon a husband with greater wealth and a noble family instead of a brawny, charmless fool whose ducal cousin was merely on a distant branch of a tree, far out of reach and unknown to him.

What she had meant was that she could no longer take the risk that she might be carrying Lachlan's bairn if she went to another man's bed. That she'd enjoyed his body with no intention of ever giving him her heart or her hand in matrimony.

Rose laid her hand on his coat sleeve. "Lachlan, I never wanted to break yer heart. Ye were my only love. What I felt for ye—what I still feel for ye—never faded or changed. Not in all the years we've been apart."

He didn't want to hear declarations from her. Not only

did he suspect they were false, but his heart no longer yearned for this woman. It yearned for another. A mysterious-eyed American hellion who had seen past the brash, graceless oaf he was to the man within. And had liked him instead of hiding him and wanting to change him.

"I wanted tae make ye my wife," he reminded Rose now, not willing to allow her to cling to pretense. "Ye told me ye needed time. I gave ye time. I pledged my love to ye. I would have given ye everything I could have, done anything tae make ye happy. But ye didnae believe a man like me could ever make enough of himself tae give ye the comfortable life of a lady ye wanted to lead."

Her fingers tightened on his sleeve. "And do ye blame me? I had no notion of where our lives would lead then. I'd already found myself close to penury from my first husband. I was too fearful to marry ye, Lachlan. George was the heir tae an earldom. His family was wealthy. He told me he loved me." She paused, emitting a bitter little laugh. "Of course, I discovered that was a lie. He never loved me at all. No man has but ye."

He pulled his sleeve from her touch, disliking the familiarity she displayed, which was wholly unwarranted. He didn't want another woman's hands on him, even with the barrier of cloth between them. There was only one woman's touch he desired, only one woman's touch he needed. And it was Madeline's.

"A fine time for ye tae realize what ye had, Lady Kelley," he said coolly, taking care to continue his formal use of her title. "I'm afraid that particular ship has set sail, never tae return."

Her brow furrowed, and although she clasped her hands at her waist, she didn't move away from him, remaining far too near. "But ye're back home in Scotland where ye belong now. Ye're the Duke of Kenross. Ye have duties tae attend.

Surely ye'll be here in Edinburgh. Our paths are destined tae cross. Dinnae try tae tell me ye cannae feel the pull between us, even after all these years."

"If ye're feeling aught, it's likely because ye've realized I'm a duke now and I'm no' beneath ye any longer," he said grimly. "Tell me, what would the earl think if he were tae learn his wife had paid a call upon another man at his hotel whilst that man's wife was awaiting him upstairs?"

At his mentioning of Madeline, Rose flinched. "So, it's true then, that ye've married the American heiress."

His mother had always been fond of saying that gossip traveled faster than a fart in a chapel. She hadn't been wrong.

"I have," he confirmed. "But I'll thank ye tae call her my duchess instead of *the American heiress*. She's worth far more than her fortune."

"Ye married her for her dowry," Rose said. "Dinnae pretend otherwise."

"I'll no' pretend anything. Nor will I pay my wife disrespect by lingering here with ye," he said, trying to keep his voice as gentle as possible.

He was beginning to think that Rose did indeed regret her decision to marry her husband as she had, instead of Lachlan. There was no contentment in her eyes—only a somber acceptance of her fate. But as he thought of the life he was beginning with Madeline, he could only feel relief and gratitude for the past.

It had made him stronger.

And aye, it had left him embittered and unwilling to trust anyone with his heart.

But it had also made it possible for him to find his own way. It had set him on the path that had led him to Madeline. And ultimately, it had shown him what true love felt like.

Love.

Aye, that was it, that feeling that had been growing inside

him, burning hot and bright, refusing to be dimmed or tamed, ever since that picnic back at Sherborne Manor.

He was in love with his wife. Only, it had taken this moment, being confronted with the past and seeing Rose for who she truly was, to make him reach that astonishing conclusion.

He turned to go without even bothering to say another word to Rose. Let her think of him what she would. She'd certainly had no qualms about leaving him in the dust years ago, and he would do the same for her now.

But she wasn't ready for him to leave. Rose hastened after him, planting herself between Lachlan and the sitting room door. She pressed her palms to his chest, staying him as she looked up at him with wide, glistening eyes that gleamed with unshed tears.

For herself? For him? He couldn't be sure, but likely the former.

"Don't go yet," she pleaded. "I'm begging ye, Lachlan. Let me explain. This is the moment I've been dreaming of for so long. It's not over between us. It never was, and it never will be. I've missed ye desperately. I think of ye every day. When I learned ye'd returned tae the city, I was overjoyed. I never stopped loving ye. I did what I felt was right because I was afraid, but I always loved ye and only ye. Grant me a chance to show ye, tae make amends for all the time we've lost."

He'd spent years believing the greatest danger he faced was allowing himself to be vulnerable again, only to realize that the true danger had been in never opening his heart to love. And now, the sole future he envisioned for himself was one with Madeline in it. Madeline at his side, in his bed, the mother of his children. His everything. Not Rose. Not anyone else.

"Rose." He took her wrists in a gentle hold, intending to pry her hands from him as he heard a gasp and caught a sudden flurry of movement in the door, which he'd somehow failed to realize had been opened a crack.

Madeline.

He'd recognize that flash of purple silk anywhere. Purple was one of her favorite colors, for it complemented her chestnut hair and dark-gray eyes perfectly.

His stomach tightened into a knot of dread. How much had she overheard? Where was she fleeing to?

He dropped Rose's wrists as if they were live coals, for they might as well have been. "Listen tae me, for I'll no' say it again. I dinnae love ye any longer, if I ever did. Now that I ken what true love is, I'm persuaded what I felt for ye was more of a youthful infatuation. I love my wife, and I have every intention of being faithful tae her and making her as happy as I'm able every day of my life. Go back tae yer husband, Rose. Dinnae seek me out again."

Her mouth fell open. Likely, he'd shocked her with his blunt speech. But he didn't give a damn. All Lachlan did care about was finding Madeline.

Before it was too late.

MADELINE FLED from the tableau she had unintentionally witnessed, tears burning her eyes, sick to her stomach as she stumbled through the lobby of the hotel, trying not to retch.

The woman Lachlan loved was here in Edinburgh. Not just here, but in their very hotel. In a private room alone with him. Touching him. Telling him she loved him.

She was beautiful. Of course she was flaxen-haired and diminutive, soft-spoken with the same lush Scottish brogue Lachlan possessed. What a couple they had made, his broad shoulders and tremendous height, his red-gold hair the perfect foil to the lustrous curls piled high on her elegant crown.

In comparison, Madeline was a gauche American who was too tall, too brash, too bold, whose dark hair was nondescript and unexceptional. Whose accent was far from lilting. She was the woman he'd married for her fortune, and the woman proclaiming her tender emotions to him in the hotel sitting room was the one he loved.

The very woman he had loved so strongly that he had not touched another woman since she had chosen to marry another man instead of him.

"Your Grace, is something amiss?" the helpful desk clerk, a pleasant young man eager to be of assistance, somewhat in awe of the duke and his American duchess who had spent the last week here in his midst, called as she passed.

She wondered if her emotions were written on her face. Lucy always told her she was far too expressive. That everyone could see plainly what she was thinking. That she could never win at a hand of poker.

Madeline summoned a smile for the clerk's benefit, aware of how painfully tight her cheeks felt. Likely, it was more of a grimace than anything else.

"Nothing is amiss at all, sir," she assured him, sailing past to the stairs beyond that would take her to the rooms she had been keeping with Lachlan.

She didn't want to see anyone. To speak to anyone. She wanted to be alone in the depths of her misery. To retreat to her den like a wounded fox and plan what she might do next. Because one thing was certain. She couldn't remain here.

Not if Lachlan returned to his former love.

She sailed on, taking the steps two at a time, nearly bowling over another guest in her haste to reach the privacy of her room so that she could burst into tears without an audience.

"Forgive me, Yer Grace," said the gentleman she had nearly collided with, bowing in deference.

He knew who she was. But then, of course he did. Everyone knew she was the Duchess of Kenross, half of the pair of wealthy American heiresses who had arrived on the shores of Great Britain. One of the daughters of Mr. William Chartrand, railroad and property magnate.

What he didn't know was that she was the other woman who loved Lachlan Macfie, Duke of Kenross. That her heart had shattered into a thousand tiny shards, like a priceless crystal goblet tossed from the lofty heights of a roof, only to smash on the pavements below.

"The fault is mine," she told the man, inwardly applauding herself for keeping her tears at bay and allowing nary a hint of a quaver into her voice.

She continued on, breathless by the time she reached the floor where her lavish rooms were located. Stifling a sob, she stuffed her key into the lock and burst over the threshold as a wave of tears threatened to overtake her.

Madeline slammed the door at her back and leaned against it for purchase, feeling as if she were a mountaineer climbing a steep slope and that, at any moment, she would slip and fall to her doom. Her heart was beating faster than she could recall it ever beating. Her mouth was drier than a desert. Her stomach was threatening to rebel, and a cold sweat had broken out on her brow.

How had everything been torn asunder with such astounding haste and ease?

The day had begun with promise. She and Lachlan had made love until the early hours of the morning when she had drifted into a dreamless, sated sleep. And she had overslept, one of her many flaws, according to Lucy. Madeline slept soundly. Thunderstorms never woke her. Commotion on the street didn't perturb her. Nothing dragged her from slumber's grip.

And so, she had risen after her husband to find him fully dressed, seeming preoccupied, a tightness in his jaw she hadn't liked. But he had reassured her that he had a small matter of business to attend to, and she had taken him at his word, thinking it must be more ducal nonsense she didn't understand that made him so pensive. She had believed him, of course. He had never given her cause to believe he was anything other than eminently trustworthy.

If she hadn't accidentally brushed against a folded missive as she dressed and sought to pick it up, she likely never would have known where he had truly gone. She certainly wouldn't have guessed. But the moment she had picked up the carefully folded note, she had been curious. The only correspondence Lachlan had been receiving had been from his solicitor and the steward at Kenross Castle. But this note had borne the flowery script of a woman—Madeline had recognized the flourishes of a feminine hand even through the thick paper.

And when she had retrieved it, even with the slightest hint of suspicion and curiosity, she had fully intended to restore it to its former place atop a Louis Quinze table.

But then it had reached her.

Perfume.

Cloying and sweet, like too many flowers in a garden all blooming at once.

No man of business would have perfumed his letter.

Dread clawing at her, she had opened it. And with a sinking heart, she had read it. Or read enough of the letter to comprehend that Lachlan's lost love had discovered he was in Edinburgh. Worse, that she had sent him a note telling him that she'd kept him *near to her heart.* Even worse, that she had signed the letter *ever and fondly yours.* But worst of all, that Lachlan had not just kept the missive a secret, he had left the room.

He had kissed Madeline tenderly and told her he had business to attend to. *Ye neednae concern yerself with it*, he'd reassured her easily in his charming brogue. *The matter is a trifling one.*

Trifling, indeed.

He'd lied.

Madeline had known it the moment the missive had fluttered from her nerveless fingers, resuming its place on the floor. She had known instantly, too, that he had gone to meet this Rose of his, the woman who had won his heart. Without even a thought for the rest of her toilette, Madeline had madly rushed from the rooms, descending to the lobby where she'd inquired after her husband with as much sangfroid as she had been able to command. Precious little, she had no doubt. The clerk had told her she might find His Grace in one of the private sitting rooms available for the use of guests of particular note.

And like a fool, she'd gone.

Not just gone, but eavesdropped, sick as she opened the door just enough to see the two of them together. Lachlan and his Rose. To overhear her dismissive words.

Ye married her for her dowry. Dinnae pretend otherwise.

A bitter laugh stole from Madeline's lips, and she clapped her hand over her mouth to stifle it. Rose, Countess of Kelley, as she had signed her name and as it would forever be emblazoned on Madeline's mind, had been quite correct in her assessment. And Madeline had been more than aware of the reason Lachlan had wanted to wed her. He'd made no secret of it.

But still, she'd been so shocked to hear a stranger baldly dismiss their marriage, and particularly after the honeymoon they had shared thus far, that Madeline had failed to hear her husband's response.

What she'd heard instead had been Rose's confession of love.

I never stopped loving ye, she'd said tenderly.

And then, the words that had been a death knell to Madeline.

Grant me a chance to show ye, tae make amends for all the time we've lost.

And instead of denying her, instead of telling her he was a married man, Lachlan had reached for Rose's dainty wrists, taking them in his big hands. And he'd called her by her given name.

Rose, he'd said.

A name Madeline would forever hate. She hadn't been able to bear another second, knowing what would happen next. Knowing that Lachlan wasn't even to blame for his feelings. He'd been clear from the start. He needed Madeline's dowry. He wanted a marriage in name only. He'd surrendered his heart to another.

And Madeline had accepted that, because at the time, she had been too prideful to realize she was already falling in love with him. But not just that, she had needed him as well. Her scheming parents had left her with precious little choice in the matter of her future. She'd had no option but to wed to save herself from her father's draconian decree and whatever dreadful spouse he would have arranged for her. No, she'd thought it better to choose a husband of her own. One she was already drawn to.

One who had been destined from the start to break her heart.

Her vision blurred. Hot tears escaped her eyes, scalding her cheeks. She bit her lip, trying to contain them. To find her composure. But she couldn't. Her misery went marrow-deep. If she had come to Scotland thinking she was falling in love with her husband, the time she had spent with Lachlan in Edinburgh had proven to her without a doubt that she hadn't merely been falling.

She was already in love.

And she loved him so much that she knew, with soul-searing despair, that she would set him free. He could return to the bosom of the woman he loved. Madeline would free him to be with his Rose. The matter of her dowry didn't concern her. She could return to London. To her mother. Or to Paris, if that was where Mother and Lucy were by now.

She was a Chartrand. Madeline would find her way. She hadn't any other choice, had she? Her other option was to remain here in Scotland as Lachlan's wife while he fell into the arms of another woman. And she knew instinctively that she wouldn't survive it. No, she had to go. To flee as fast and as far as she was able. It was the only solution for everyone involved.

Suddenly, the door rattled at her back.

Someone was trying to enter, but she must have locked it upon her return without realizing, so caught up in her anguish. Likely, it was one of the porters or perhaps even one of the maids, intent upon serving the Duke and Duchess of Kenross.

She swiped at her tears, taking a deep breath as she struggled to compose herself. "I don't require any assistance, thank you."

"Madeline."

It was Lachlan's voice, low, velvet-soft, and far too beloved.

She closed her eyes. "I'm indisposed."

A lie. She would have felt remorse for it, but he'd clearly felt none at deceiving her earlier so that he could meet his love.

"Madeline, I need tae speak with ye."

The door gave another shudder.

"I don't want to speak at the moment," she said with as much calm as she could manage.

"I saw ye at the door," he said, with grim meaning. "I know what ye think ye heard. But I can explain. Let me in, lass."

Lass.

She loved when he called her that.

Once, it had caused her great consternation. She'd thought him irritatingly familiar. How quickly her opinion of him had altered. How easily she'd fallen beneath his charming spell.

"No," she said, steeling herself against his appeal.

The door shook with greater force. "I'll break it down. Is that what ye wish?"

"I wish to be left alone."

"Stand back." The door rattled again. "I'm going tae kick the bluidy bugger in."

"Lachlan."

Surely he wouldn't? This was a fine hotel. The finest in Edinburgh. He was a duke. He—

Thump. Thump. Thump.

The door was jumping now. Oh dear Lord.

"Move away, lass," he warned.

Finally comprehending that he did indeed intend to do as he had promised, Madeline fled across the room.

"Have ye moved?"

"Yes," she called.

It was almost comical. She ought to have simply unlocked the door for him. But her mind was scattered. She wasn't thinking properly.

Crack.

Crash.

Thwack.

The door opened with a violent burst, bouncing off the plaster wall behind it.

And there her husband stood like an avenging Scots warrior of old, wild-eyed, tall, muscled, and unfairly handsome. She had to swallow hard against a rush of longing and ball her hands into fists at her sides, digging her nails into her palms to distract herself from the tears that threatened to fall.

"I'm sorry, *mo gràidh.* Can ye forgive me?" He was breathing heavily, his broad chest rising and falling, his blue eyes on her. Searing. Asking.

"You lied to me," she said.

"Aye, I did by keeping who I intended tae meet from ye." He crossed the threshold, closing the damaged door behind him, and started across the room to her. "I should have been honest. I was shocked tae receive a note from her. I wasnae thinking clearly."

He stopped before her, towering over Madeline, more intense than she had ever seen him, nary a trace of the humor so often sparkling in his eyes and tipping up the corners of his sensual lips.

"Of course you weren't thinking clearly," she forced herself to say. "The woman you love sent you a letter, wanting to meet you. Naturally, you ran to her."

"Nay." He shook his head, jaw clenched as he scrubbed a hand over it. "I told her I wouldnae meet her, but then she arrived at the hotel and a porter came tae tell me a guest was awaiting me below. I knew I needed tae see her, but I didnae want tae trouble ye with it. I realize that was a mistake."

"It wasn't a mistake." A rush of sadness hit Madeline, so overwhelming that it nearly robbed her of the capacity for speech. She forged on, needing to get the words out. "You were torn between me and the woman you love. But you needn't be. I won't stand in the way of your happiness, Lachlan."

His brow furrowed. "What are ye saying, lass?"

"I'm saying that I overheard what she told you. That she loves you." Madeline stopped and swallowed hard, tamping down the hot rush of tears before continuing. "And I know you love her too. I'll take the train back to York. Perhaps we can have our marriage annulled. I know you need my dowry for your castle—"

"Ye're leaving me?" he interrupted, looking as shocked as he sounded. "Ye want tae end our marriage?"

She never wanted to leave him. But she loved him too much to stay. Loved him too much to force him to remain trapped in a marriage with her when he loved someone else.

"Yes," she said, her voice breaking on the lone word as tears slipped down her cheeks. "I'm leaving you."

"Nay." He took her hands in his, his grip firm but tender. "Ye're no' leaving me. I won't let ye."

She tried to tug her hands free, but he was stubborn and stronger than she was, and she gave up for the moment. "I have to. I can't stay and watch you with her. It will break me."

"Lass, I dinnae love her, and I verra much doubt she loves me. I dinnae think she kens what love is." He gave her hands a gentle squeeze. "And as for ye taking a train tae York, ye had better secure two tickets. Because ye're no' going anywhere without me."

Madeline blinked furiously, trying to clear the tears from her vision. Lachlan was a beloved blur before her. "You...you don't love her?"

Suddenly, nothing made sense.

"I cannae love her," he said softly. "Because my heart already belongs to someone else."

Her knees threatened to give out. "What do you mean by that, Lachlan?"

The tears had stopped, and she blinked again, his handsome face no longer indistinct but clear. His bright-blue gaze burned into hers.

"*Mo gràidh*," he said tenderly. "Ye asked me what it meant before, and I lied tae ye. It doesnae mean *wife*. It means *my love*. I love ye, Madeline. I love ye, and I'm the world's biggest arse for no' telling ye until I'm about tae lose ye."

My love.

Mo gràidh.

I love ye.

Madeline was dizzied as the words sank into her mind. Lachlan loved her?

"But that's impossible," she protested weakly.

"On the contrary," he said softly, smiling down at her. "It's very possible. I dinnae ken when it happened. All I *do* ken is that I was wrong tae think the greatest mistake I could ever make was falling in love. Wrong tae think it was more important tae guard my heart than listen tae it. I love ye more than words can possibly express, lass. I love ye so much, it terrifies me. I love *ye*, no' anyone else, and if ye leave, I'll follow. I'll follow ye tae New York or London or Paris or wherever ye go. Ye dinnae have tae love me in return. Heaven knows I dinnae deserve it after all this. But please, *mo gràidh*, please dinnae leave me."

As he finished his fervent declaration, new tears were stinging Madeline's eyes. Not tears of sadness, however. Tears of pure, unadulterated joy welling up inside her.

"Do you mean it?" she asked, blinking again so that she could see his expression.

And all the love reflected there.

For her alone.

"I've never meant anything more, lass." He brought her hands to his lips, pressing a kiss to each one. "Please tell me ye'll forgive me and that you willnae leave me."

He still thought she would leave him? Taking a train anywhere was the furthest notion from her mind.

"Of course I won't leave you. I thought it would be what you wanted after I saw the two of you together."

"I'm a fool." He pulled her into his chest, and she went willingly, burrowing into the solid strength of him. "I'm so sorry I made ye think, even for a moment, that I would choose anyone else over ye. Ye're all I want, lass. All I need. I love ye."

She wrapped her arms around his neck, happiness bursting inside her like the sun reappearing after a terrible storm. "I love you too, Lachlan."

"Ye do?" He stared down at her, looking astounded.

Madeline smiled, overwhelmed with emotion. "I do."

"Ye love me." He was grinning at her now, boyish and unabashed in his joy.

And she was grinning back. "I love you."

She wanted to shout it from the rooftop of the hotel. To let all Edinburgh know. To tell the world. She wanted everyone to know that he was hers, and she was his.

Forever.

Lachlan kissed her, fast and hard. "I'm going tae carry ye across this room tae the bed and make love tae ye, lass."

Warmth pooled between her thighs. "Yes." Briefly, she thought of the damage he'd done to the door, the broken lock. "What will we tell the hotel staff about the door?"

His grin deepened, his eyes crinkling at the corners. "I'll tell them the truth. That I'm a great big, hulking beast and I dinnae know my own strength."

"You are big and strong," she agreed, rising on her toes to press her lips to his in a swift kiss. "But not a beast. Never that."

"I'm glad ye dinnae think so, *mo gràidh*." He swept her into his arms with ease, as if she weighed no more than a sack of flour.

"How could I?" She caressed his cheek as he made good on his word, carrying her across the room to the bed. "You saved me."

"Nay, lass," he corrected, looking down at her with such raw, naked love that it took her breath away. "It's *ye* who saved *me*."

He lowered her to the rumpled bedclothes, and when he flipped up her skirts and began kissing a path of fire along her inner thigh, Madeline decided not to argue the point.

For they'd saved each other, in more ways than one.

EPILOGUE

CASTLE KENROSS, EIGHT YEARS LATER

The lawn at Castle Kenross was buzzing like a hive laden with bees. The happy laughter of children filled the air, along with the cheerful barking of hounds who were bounding about in the grass with the lads and lasses.

The Duke and Duchess of Bradford's eldest lad, Percy, tagged the Marquess and Marchioness of Dorset's daughter. Young Lydia tripped over her flounced hems in her determination to catch the Blakemoor lad, Arthur, who promptly laughed at her. Fanny, daughter to the Earl and Countess of Rexingham, stuck out her foot at just the right moment and caused young Arthur to fall. Lydia seized the opportunity to tag poor Arthur, who really rather had deserved his comeuppance, and the lad lurched to his feet, chasing after the golden-haired daughter of Lord and Lady Wilton, Violet. From the lowest limb of a tree, Lachlan and Madeline's eldest son, Alastair, watched the lively game unfolding, Decker and Lady Jo's son at his side, feet swinging below his perch.

Alastair had Lachlan's red-gold hair and his mother's gray eyes, and every time Lachlan looked upon his son, his chest swelled with fatherly pride. He'd been a huge bairn, just as

Lachlan had. Their daughter, Catriona—named after his sainted mother—had been petite at birth, but what she'd lacked in size, she more than made up for in personality. As evidenced now as she clambered up the tree after her older brother, her fat red braid cascading down her determined little back.

"It's wonderful to see all the children playing together, so carefree, isn't it?" Madeline asked at Lachlan's side.

He tore his gaze from the children and took in the sight of his beautiful wife, whose belly was swelled round with their next bairn. "I dinnae think it's possible tae be happier than this," he said honestly.

It had taken them two grueling years to restore Kenross Castle to its former glory and a fair bit of Madeline's tremendous dowry. But when they had finally finished their task, they'd begun an annual tradition of inviting their closest friends and their families for a summer house party. Each year, the ranks swelled as couples had more children, bringing additional joy and laughter to the once quiet, crumbling halls of the castle. The husbands and wives remained loyal friends, continuing their devotion to their cause with the Lady's Suffrage Society.

Around them, a massive picnic had been laid, all the couples scattered about in contentment as their offspring played with unashamed delight. Lachlan was reclining on a blanket, long legs crossed at his booted ankles, so stuffed full of salad and ginger beer that he didn't think he'd be able to move for at least a half hour. The repast had been marvelous, and he'd been ravenous as usual.

"Feeling full?"

At his wife's arch tone, Lachlan gave her a sheepish look. "How can ye tell?"

"Because your eyes are always bigger than your stomach is," she told him primly.

And she was right.

Aye, his beloved was right about a lot of things.

Most things, actually. But he had no intention of telling her that. She'd crow about it for years.

"Ye know me well, *mo gràidh*," he said instead, swooping in for a swift kiss despite the fact that they were surrounded by friends and wily children.

Madeline smiled, her eyes dancing in that way of hers that never failed to make him long to take her in his arms and carry her away to the nearest bedroom. "Aye, that I do, *mo chridhe*."

"I cannae help my love of lettuce," he said, patting his flat stomach. "Just as I cannae help my love of a beautiful American hellion who stole my heart and made it hers."

She sent him a flirtatious wink, rubbing the pale silk stretched over her burgeoning belly. "And you'll not be getting it back."

"Aye, it's yers forever, just as I am." Lachlan lowered his head to her ear, inhaling her sweet scent, keeping his voice soft so that it wouldn't carry. "Now, do ye think the two of us might slip away tae the castle without any of the wee ones taking note? I find I'm still hungry after all."

Hungry for his beautiful wife.

Aye, he'd never have his fill of Madeline.

Madeline bit her lip, obviously trying to quell her wicked smile. "What about our guests?"

"I'll no' have them join us if ye dinnae mind," he said teasingly. "The husbands can pleasure their own wives at their leisure. One wife is all I can handle."

Madeline chuckled. "Where did I find you?"

He kissed the hollow behind her ear that he knew drove her mad, gratified when she shivered. "Ye found me at a house party in York, of all places. I spilled champagne on yer train and trampled on it, and it was love at first sight."

"Oh yes," she murmured, casting him a naughty look that promised all manner of sensual delights. "How could I forget?" She leaned closer to him. "I'll meet you in the solar in five minutes."

She was perfect for him, his duchess. In every way.

Lachlan grinned. "I hope ye arenae wearing any drawers."

Madeline sent him a coquettish look. "You'll have to find out for yourself."

Och. She was going to kill him. And he'd love every minute of the sweet, sensual torture.

It was Lachlan's turn to wink now. "There's nothing I'd like more, lass." He leaned nearer again to murmur in her ear, "And if ye are wearing them, I'll tear them off ye with my teeth."

She made a soft humming sound, turning to him with a wicked smile. "Promise?"

"Aye, lass. That's a promise."

THANK you for reading Madeline and Lachlan's happily ever after! I hope you enjoyed their steamy, bantering, emotional path to love. Many of you first met Lachlan in *Lady Wallflower* and have been asking for his story ever since—thank you for loving him as much as I do! This may be farewell for now to Dukes Most Wanted, but there's far more to come from me. Read on for an excerpt from *How to Love a Dangerous Rogue*, a spicy enemies-to-lovers Regency romance with age gap, danger, and all the swoon.

Please stay in touch! The only way to be sure you'll know what's next from me is to sign up for my newsletter here: http://eepurl.com/dyJSar. Please join my reader group for early excerpts, cover reveals, and more here: https://www.facebook.com/groups/scarlettscottreaders. And if you're in the mood to chat all things steamy historical romance and read a different book together each month, join my book club, Dukes Do It Hotter right here: https://www.facebook.com/groups/hotdukes because we're having a whole lot of fun! Now, on to that excerpt...

How to Love a Dangerous Rogue
Royals & Renegades Book One

Lady Tansy Francis has been a loyal lady-in-waiting for most of her life. In the eyes of the *ton*, she has come to London for the formal betrothal announcement of the princess who is like a sister to her. But secretly, Tansy has become caught up in the plans for a revolution in her homeland. She finds herself with no choice but to join forces with the last person she should ever trust, a coldhearted man who is feared by many: the king to whom the princess is about to announce her betrothal.

King Maximilian of Varros has a reputation that precedes him as a brutal, callous ruler who has stopped at nothing to claim his throne. After many long years of war, he has forged peace in his kingdom. But that peace is being threatened, and he'll burn everything and everyone to the ground to save it. Only a few obstacles are standing in his path, and one of them happens to be a fearless lady-in-waiting he can't stop wanting.

Tansy's allegiance is to the princess, but King Maximilian has no qualms about seizing whatever he desires, consequences be damned. With the fires of revolution lit and chaos swirling around them, their passion is forbidden and yet impossible to resist. Trapped between old loyalties and new longings, Tansy has to make the most difficult choice of all—risk her heart for a dangerous rogue...or watch as he marries her best friend.

<u>Chapter One</u>

THE KING of Varros had arrived.

The approach of the carriage in the streets below had warned her, along with the rustle of frantic movement in the hall outside the chamber, the raised voices, the hastening footsteps. She hadn't expected him.

Not now. Not today. Not yet.

"Perdition," Tansy swore, then added another vicious Boritanian oath for good measure as she plumped the pillows beneath the counterpane on the princess's bed, a fine sheen of sweat on her brow.

She didn't want to see the king without Princess Anastasia acting as a necessary barrier. But it would seem, like much of her life, Tansy didn't have a choice in the matter.

For in that moment, the door opened to admit *him*.

She moved away from the bed instantly, as if the empty piece of furniture had singed her hand, guilt warring with trepidation within her.

King Maximilian was obscenely tall and broad, seeming to take up half the chamber with his entrance. His size, in this instance, was fortuitous, as it meant the guard in the hall couldn't spy the empty bed in which the princess was meant to be reclining as an invalid, nor the pillows that were a poor imitation of her feminine form.

The door clicked closed, and Tansy watched as the king raised a massive paw to latch it in place, trapping her with him. *Alone.*

He turned to her slowly, his brown eyes dark and unreadable, mouth grim and unsmiling. "You've a vicious tongue, Lady Tansy."

His English bore the traces of a Varrosian accent but was otherwise flawless.

Sweet Deus above, had he heard her cursing? How? She had been muttering to herself, not shouting. Tansy felt light-headed at the prospect, knowing full well that he could punish her for daring to utter such an oath in the presence of the king.

Belatedly, she remembered herself, dipping into a curtsy. "Your Majesty."

"Repeat it," he ordered curtly.

Tansy had just straightened to her full height, which wasn't considerable under any circumstances, and most certainly not when in the presence of King Maximilian, who towered over her as mightily as any mountain. But she dipped again, offering him a protracted curtsy, making extra effort.

"Your Majesty," she said.

"Not that." He flicked his hand in a dismissive gesture. "What came before it."

Curse the devil. He *had* heard. She didn't dare repeat the Boritanian oath. Literally translated to English, it meant *May God rot your cock.*

Decidedly not the sort of thing one said to a king, particularly one as menacing and imposing as the monarch before her.

"I beg your pardon, Your Majesty," she offered, bowing her head in a show of humility that she hoped would appease him. "I said nothing else."

He had drawn nearer. Soundlessly, which was impressive for a man so large in stature. With her head bowed, she saw the perfectly gleaming black boots—as immense as every other part of him—a mere foot away. The hair on the back of her neck rose.

"You dare to lie to me?" he demanded, his voice deceptively low.

It was the quietness that frightened her most. The stories of the horrors King Maximilian had visited upon his enemies were legion. He had battled for years to emerge the victor and assume the throne that was rightfully his, sparing no one.

Ruthless.

Pitiless.

Unfeeling.

Those were a scant few of the whispers Tansy had heard about him.

"I would never presume to lie to you, Your Majesty," she fibbed, head still bent, praying he would cease toying with her.

"Look at me, Lady Tansy."

She didn't want to. Particularly not given the king's troubling proximity. So near that she could detect his scent, spice and musk with a hint of leather and citrus. A pleasant scent. Altogether not one she would have expected of a man like him, but she had never previously been near enough to take note. She supposed it stood to reason that brutal warriors might smell as lovely as anyone else.

Tansy took a deep, shaky breath. "Forgive me, Your—"

"I said, *look at me*," he interrupted, enunciating each of the words as sharply as if he wielded a whip.

She lifted her head and wished she hadn't. He was even closer than she had supposed, presiding over her like one of the old gods her ancestors had worshiped. Fierce and fearsome, his face a collection of angular blades—wide jaw, high cheekbones, a stern nose. A fine scar marred the skin above one of his slashing brows, a shocking hint of a past vulnerability. His black hair brushed over broad shoulders, twin patches of silver at his temples. He had amber flecks in the dark-brown depths of his eyes, and his mouth was almost cruel to look upon, sensual and full lips so harsh and unyielding.

And then those lips moved. "Say it again, Lady Tansy."

She swallowed hard, her stomach knotting. Now she had done it. All these years of avoiding the wrath of the usurper Boritanian King Gustavson, and one foolish oath had ruined her.

In a quiet voice, she repeated the curse and then waited, shoulders tense, for a blow. For a cuff to the side of the head for her insolence. Everyone knew how vicious King Maximilian was.

"Are you a sorceress, madam?" he growled, the tone of his voice low and deep.

The question took her by surprise.

Confusion made her brow furrow. "Of course not, Your Majesty."

"Good, for I do not wish for my cock to rot off."

She stared at him, aghast. King Maximilian did not jest. Did he? No, it simply wasn't possible. And there was nary a hint of levity in his immovable countenance. Was there? The man could have been carved from marble, though she very much doubted he would be cool and smooth to the touch. Something told her he would be quite hot.

At the errant and most unwelcome thought, she nearly choked. The result was a strangled sound that was most impolite.

"Are you well?" he asked, his gaze narrowing.

No, she was not well. She was alone with a merciless tyrant who would soon be marrying the princess who had become like a sister to her over the years she had spent as Princess Anastasia's lady-in-waiting. Tansy couldn't bear to hold his gaze. Her head dropped, her gaze falling to the carpet.

"I beg Your Majesty's forgiveness," she mumbled, still stricken by her lapse.

How could she have been so foolish as to exclaim the vile oath aloud?

She blamed the hours she had spent waiting for Princess Anastasia's return, fretting and fearing on her behalf.

"I asked if you are well," he reminded pointedly.

She was aware of him shifting; there was a rustle of fabric, his long arm stretching toward her slowly.

Would he strike her now, then?

"Very well, thank you, Your Majesty," she managed, scarcely moving her lips.

"Hmm," was all he said, his voice fashioned of steel and ice. And then his finger was on her chin, rough and firm and yet surprisingly gentle, urging it upward. Making her meet his gaze again. "I won't hurt you, if that is what you fear. Does King Gustavson strike the women in his court?"

The bloodied lashes she had tended on the princess's back rose in Tansy's mind, and she had to bite back the bile rising in her throat. She should lie, for the tale was not hers to tell. But with his fathomless gaze holding her in thrall, she couldn't seem to find the words. Still, she needed to say something. The king had spoken to her. Had asked her a question.

"I—" she began, only for his finger to settle in the bow of her upper lip, staying further explanation.

"You've answered me well enough," he interrupted.

As quickly as he had reached for her, he withdrew his touch, before spinning on his heel and stalking toward the door. He unlatched and wrenched it open. Then, he strode out, closing it smartly at his back, somehow taking the air from the room with him.

Tansy stared at the paneled door, holding her breath.

The only sounds were more muffled voices and booted

footsteps disappearing down the hall, both finally supplanted by the rhythmic ticking of a mantel clock. The jangling of tack interrupted, rising from the street below. And still the door remained closed.

Tansy waited, lip tingling where King Maximilian had laid his finger.

Want more? Get *How to Love a Dangerous Rogue* now!

DON'T MISS SCARLETT'S OTHER ROMANCES!

Complete Book List
HISTORICAL ROMANCE

Heart's Temptation
A Mad Passion (Book One)
Rebel Love (Book Two)
Reckless Need (Book Three)
Sweet Scandal (Book Four)
Restless Rake (Book Five)
Darling Duke (Book Six)
The Night Before Scandal (Book Seven)

Wicked Husbands
Her Errant Earl (Book One)
Her Lovestruck Lord (Book Two)
Her Reformed Rake (Book Three)
Her Deceptive Duke (Book Four)
Her Missing Marquess (Book Five)
Her Virtuous Viscount (Book Six)

League of Dukes
Nobody's Duke (Book One)
Heartless Duke (Book Two)
Dangerous Duke (Book Three)
Shameless Duke (Book Four)
Scandalous Duke (Book Five)
Fearless Duke (Book Six)

Notorious Ladies of London
Lady Ruthless (Book One)
Lady Wallflower (Book Two)
Lady Reckless (Book Three)
Lady Wicked (Book Four)
Lady Lawless (Book Five)
Lady Brazen (Book 6)

Unexpected Lords
The Detective Duke (Book One)
The Playboy Peer (Book Two)
The Millionaire Marquess (Book Three)
The Goodbye Governess (Book Four)

Dukes Most Wanted
Forever Her Duke (Book One)
Forever Her Marquess (Book Two)
Forever Her Rake (Book Three)
Forever Her Earl (Book Four)
Forever Her Viscount (Book Five)
Forever Her Scot (Book Six)

The Wicked Winters
Wicked in Winter (Book One)
Wedded in Winter (Book Two)
Wanton in Winter (Book Three)

Wishes in Winter (Book 3.5)
Willful in Winter (Book Four)
Wagered in Winter (Book Five)
Wild in Winter (Book Six)
Wooed in Winter (Book Seven)
Winter's Wallflower (Book Eight)
Winter's Woman (Book Nine)
Winter's Whispers (Book Ten)
Winter's Waltz (Book Eleven)
Winter's Widow (Book Twelve)
Winter's Warrior (Book Thirteen)
A Merry Wicked Winter (Book Fourteen)

The Sinful Suttons
Sutton's Spinster (Book One)
Sutton's Sins (Book Two)
Sutton's Surrender (Book Three)
Sutton's Seduction (Book Four)
Sutton's Scoundrel (Book Five)
Sutton's Scandal (Book Six)
Sutton's Secrets (Book Seven)

Rogue's Guild
Her Ruthless Duke (Book One)
Her Dangerous Beast (Book Two)
Her Wicked Rogue (Book 3)

Royals and Renegades
How to Love a Dangerous Rogue (Book One)
How to Tame a Dissolute Prince (Book Two)

Sins and Scoundrels
Duke of Depravity
Prince of Persuasion

Marquess of Mayhem
Sarah
Earl of Every Sin
Duke of Debauchery
Viscount of Villainy

Sins and Scoundrels Box Set Collections
Volume 1
Volume 2

The Wicked Winters Box Set Collections
Collection 1
Collection 2
Collection 3
Collection 4

Wicked Husbands Box Set Collections
Volume 1
Volume 2

Notorious Ladies of London Box Set Collections
Volume 1

Stand-alone Novella
Lord of Pirates

CONTEMPORARY ROMANCE
Love's Second Chance
Reprieve (Book One)
Perfect Persuasion (Book Two)
Win My Love (Book Three)

Coastal Heat
Loved Up (Book One)

ABOUT THE AUTHOR

USA Today and Amazon bestselling author Scarlett Scott writes steamy Victorian and Regency romance with strong, intelligent heroines and sexy alpha heroes. She lives in Pennsylvania and Maryland with her Canadian husband, their adorable identical twins, a demanding diva of a dog, and one zany cat.

A self-professed literary junkie and nerd, she loves reading anything, but especially romance novels, poetry, and Middle English verse. Catch up with her on her website https://scarlettscottauthor.com. Hearing from readers never fails to make her day.

Scarlett's complete book list and information about upcoming releases can be found at https://scarlettscottauthor.com.

Connect with Scarlett! You can find her here:
Join Scarlett Scott's reader group on Facebook for early excerpts, giveaways, and a whole lot of fun!
Sign up for her newsletter here
https://www.tiktok.com/@authorscarlettscott

facebook.com/AuthorScarlettScott

x.com/scarscoromance

instagram.com/scarlettscottauthor

bookbub.com/authors/scarlett-scott

amazon.com/Scarlett-Scott/e/B004NW8N2I

pinterest.com/scarlettscott